✂
F77f

THE
FORBIDDEN
BEAST

JOHN FORRESTER

BRADBURY PRESS   NEW YORK

Bradbury Press, Inc.
An Affiliate of Macmillan, Inc.
866 Third Avenue, New York, N.Y. 10022
Collier Macmillan Canada, Inc.

Printed and bound in the United States of America
10 9 8 7 6 5 4 3 2 1
The text of this book is set in 12 pt. Times Roman.

Library of Congress Cataloging-in-Publication Data
Forrester, John, date.
    The forbidden beast / by John Forrester.
        p.   cm.
    Summary: A master computer called New Think, or
the Forbidden Beast, decides to destroy all life on earth,
but first accepts a challenge to come to visit it to find
out what experiences organic life has to offer.
    ISBN 0-02-735410-5
    [1. Fantasy.]   I. Title.
PZ7.F7715Fo   1988
[Fic] — dc19   88-2643   CIP   AC

TO BRANDI AND DUSTI

CONTENTS

MAJOR CHARACTERS

RYLAND LANGSTROM — The eminent geneticist on Luna who turned outlaw years ago. Like his wife, Tava, he committed his career to saving Old Earth's lost species of animals and plants.

TAVA LANGSTROM — An equally talented biologist, she escaped to Old Earth fifteen years ago, leaving her husband and infant twins behind. In her laboratory on Bestiary Mountain, she has successfully restored many creatures from Old Earth.

TAMARA — Sixteen-year-old daughter of Ryland and Tava, she is bright and resourceful, and a gifted telepath.

DREWYN — Tamara's twin, he escaped with her to Old Earth to find their mother.

SARAJ — An organic-electronic Overone, a product of Luna's technology, she escaped with the Langstrom twins and is Drewyn's love.

MARIAN LYTAL — Beloved companion of Ryland Langstrom and, unknown to him, the best Overone designer ever built.

JARIC — On Luna, he was Drewyn's best friend and an outstanding young pilot. He was captured by the Overones, rulers of the moon, and damaged in their interrogation. He escaped to Old Earth, but has betrayed Bestiary Mountain and kidnapped Tamara.

KANA — Half lynx, half human boy, he is a product of Tava's laboratory. Though admired for his mind and grace, he longed for Tava to return his love for her. Frustrated, he betrayed his creator to the Gorid. Then, astonished by his mistreatment by his new master, he sought safety at the Sorceror's camp.

GORID MALCOLM HAWXHURST — Once a geneticist and leader on the moon, he established his domain on Old Earth where for many years he struggled against Tava. Then, to his great surprise, Jaric seized his command and he was forced to throw himself upon Tava's mercy.

THE SORCEROR — Part human and part animal, he is a trading partner of the Gorid and a beast with his own powers and plans.

THE ROUND BEAST — Secretive and wise, living in the darkness of its chamber beneath Bestiary Mountain, this being must choose the form it will take in its escape.

THE FORBIDDEN BEAST — Master of Lunar Overones, this supreme electronic intelligence has accepted the Round Beast's challenge to visit Earth in order to experience the green planet's pleasures. Also called New Think. The confrontation between the Round Beast and the Forbidden Beast will determine Old Earth's fate.

1
KANA'S TRIAL

Dawn was breaking over the Sorceror's mountain. Dense white pines blanketed the middle slopes, and in this hour they stood windless and still. Slowly, one ray at a time, cold early sunlight found its way down into the green shadows. And there, crouched soundlessly on the sweet-smelling pine straw, Kana waited, afraid to move.

Panz was very close. The whole mountain was his territory, so he had the confidence of home ground. It was unthinkable to him that the blue-furred cat could appear and threaten to take Talia for himself. Before the sun grew white and high, Panz was certain, he would drag the outsider's lifeless carcass to the council rock. Then the Sorceror would see how foolish he'd been to waste time on a stranger. And Talia — she'd wait for Panz for a while after this. He might forgive her in some far later moon, but she would pay first, and keep on paying. Panz's muscles rippled beneath his loose skin. He drew his lips back over his gums and exposed his sharp teeth in anxiety. Then he smiled, ready. Just let the intruder move.

Half lynx and half human, Kana was the creation of the woman Tava in her genetic laboratory. She had taken her own genes and spliced them with those of a wild lynx, creating and then raising Kana. He was unique, mateless, and until now, until Talia, cursed with his loneliness.

He was Tava's idea of a helper — sentry and soldier, lab assistant, and finally companion. Never mind his misery, his hopeless love for her. Finally, he'd had all he could take, and he'd betrayed his creator to the Gorid. Then had come the long nightmare of mistreatment at the hands of his new master. In the final humiliation, the Gorid had run him with the pack of experimental humanoid-hounds, treated him as sport-prey for the Great Hunt Chase, the contest among warriors.

Kana blushed to think of it now. Every move he'd made to trust another had been wrong. But before that last horrible chase he had come to this mountain for the tournaments and games of beasts, and for the first time he'd met other cat-humans like himself. Panz, Talia, and the others were gray-furred, quick with intelligence, and they were third generation in natural births. Their grandparents had been products of genetics laboratories like himself; they, however, owed their existence to the Sorceror. From the first minute, Kana had hoped to live with them.

During the long chase, and his journey of survival afterward, Kana had been sustained by the images of Talia in his mind. On his return, to erase even the hint of a scent trail, he had taken a hundred-mile loop south, following rivers and swamps, swimming more than walking, until he was satisfied that the hunter Jaric and his hounds had long given up. Finally, Kana had reached the Sorceror's camp at the base of this mountain, and to his astonishment he'd been made welcome — especially by Talia. For weeks after, he studied at the Sorceror's feet, learning how this new feline-human community had been created and led, and learning to practice meditation and to prepare for spirit journeys.

Kana roamed the cliffs with Talia and let his feelings grow without words, as she seemed to do. Only Panz did not accept him. Kana knew all about rivalry with humans — through his failure in the competition for affection with Tava's human children — but he hadn't known how such things were resolved here. Finally, last night, the Sorceror had told him.

Now his cat's hearing picked out the tiniest scratching of claw on rock, the rhythmic, nervous motion of his enemy. It was upslope, perhaps five seconds' run, and so slight it was surely an unintended sound.

The ground-breeze of the night had been from valley to ridge, and it would soon be shifting. But at any moment Panz might smell him — he had to if Kana stayed. So, even though Panz held the slope, it was time to risk running over the forest floor.

Kana made a blurred dash toward Panz. Better to break this awful waiting that was draining his strength and start the fight. Straight into the memory of the claw-click Kana ran, eyes slitted and angry, ears flat, neck fur bristling. He broke a thin dry pine branch with a sharp crack at the three-second mark. Panz would now likely be waiting for him above. Dashing to the right, Kana pulled himself up the grade in long, loping

strides, slicing through pine shadows like a spirit cat.
Two seconds later he stopped and stared left. Panz, on
the same level, heard him only at that moment and
faced him in surprise.

The two furious cats ran together with frenzied speed
and tore each other's fur in flying patches as they raked
claws down rich coats and thin, sensitive catskin. Each
frothing mouth was open and darting around and around,
seeking a death-lock atop the enemy's neck. But each
mouth found only a shoulder. Latched in tight with
bloody talons, Kana and Panz rolled downslope between the trees as one heaving and gasping ball.

When they crashed into the huge, half-open trunk
of an ancient seed tree and jammed inside against the
dry, shedding wood, neither could quite reach the delicate jugular beneath the other's jawline. Nor could
they quite clamp down on the other's thick and straining
neck. Their teeth banged together and their eyes joined
for an unsettling instant of hatred and understanding.
Weakened by this connecting moment, they jerked
violently away from each other.

Then they circled, crouching and spitting, each emit-
ting the low death-rattle growl that announced they
didn't care. Suddenly Kana leapt high into the air over
Panz, spinning his unsheathed claws desperately as he
fell. He felt his enemy's back fur tear and knew he'd
opened a long and terrible wound. Blood poured down
both sides of Panz's body, and he shivered as he circled
and groaned. Now his rattle had risen in tenor, his tail
was twitching with fear, and Kana saw the look of the
rabbit in his eyes. He waited, letting Panz bleed, and
circled faster. When Panz was dizzy, Kana batted his

face aside and set his teeth in the soft white fur of his throat. Panz trembled and tried not to move. Kana heaved for breath, nearly choking on the mouthful of hot fur, but he did not close. One yank, and it would be over. Talia would be his. But there was something about this fighting cat he didn't want to kill. It was that quick sharing of the eyes. It was the knowing that had come.

Slowly, Kana twisted Panz downward to the pine straw, pinning him tightly, holding him upside down. Panz's belly was exposed to Kana's rear claws now, and Kana tapped a claw-point on his thinnest skin, almost idly, and felt his belly heave.

If he let his adversary go, Panz might still kill him. Yet somehow Kana wanted to do it, and he did. He stood back, waiting, but Panz didn't rise. He lay over on his side, panting, eyes half closed, with the blood pouring out of his back and pooling on the matted straw.

"Is it over?" Kana said.

"Yes," Panz whispered. "Over."

Kana dashed his front paw into the soft earth beneath the pine needles and flung dirt behind him. Again and again he made this long scratching mark, unable to stop, marking ground, letting an instinctive self have freedom, and savoring for a few moments more his victim's helplessness. Kana felt his oldest catbrain calling for the kill, even now.

But he was more than cat, and his thoughts began to clear as he felt sharp pains all over his back and deep in his shoulder.

"You did well," an aged voice said. He spun around

to see the Sorceror and Talia standing softly behind him.

Kana was speechless. ''I didn't finish him,'' he finally said.

''Why not?''

''It's not necessary,'' he replied, looking again at Panz. His opponent's eyes were closed now, his breathing quick and shallow, his hind legs beginning to twitch.

''Perhaps I could save him,'' the Sorceror said. ''Shall I try?''

''Yes, please,'' Kana said.

And the Sorceror walked forward, knelt gracefully with his tall frame, and put his padded hand gently onto Panz's head. Almost instantly the breathing relaxed, and in another minute the twitching and jerking stopped. Slowly, the aged feline Sorceror touched each of Panz's wounds, and lastly he opened the wounded warrior's eyes with his fingers. ''He will live,'' the Sorceror said. ''Now come here.''

Kana knelt beside him, and the Sorceror put his other hand on Kana's aching shoulder. With the touch, Kana felt a hot glow inside his muscles and bones that traveled in soft waves through his body. He felt drowsy and warm, and quickly the pains were gone.

Then the Sorceror and Kana stood and Talia stepped close. The Sorceror joined their hands beneath his own. ''You survived in the wilderness, Kana,'' he said, ''and prevailed in this fight. These were the tests of instinct and strength and of your courage. You have also studied with me and learned much, and for some reason you spared this good man. These are tests of ritual and reason.

"You are a worthy young man, Kana, and I give you and Talia my blessing."

Kana wanted to speak, but his mouth was dry, and his eyes were watery.

The Sorceror smiled, and Kana saw the puma lines in his old face. "Come to me in the morning," said the Sorceror.

Kana and Talia walked together up the grade through the grove of trees. They didn't speak, but they moved together, touching, feeling each other's heat. They drank together from a pool of clear blue water, then lay on the rock ledge beside it.

The morning sun was high and warm, and Kana slept. Much later, he and Talia walked to a higher ledge, where he discovered his cuts were healed. He still had the strange warmth inside and still felt sleepy.

By nightfall the two cats had come to a small cave that Talia had lined with green pine boughs and stocked with food. It faced the fading mountain sunset, and they watched in silence as broad varnished strokes of red melted into deep purple.

Kana went to sleep thinking of his life here, among these cat-persons, and of Talia. But he dreamed of the Round Beast. Thrashing awake in the darkness, he was comforted by Talia, who stroked his back softly and drew him down inside her warm spell. Kana was grateful, and more than willing. But when he closed his eyes the Round Beast came before him again, reaching in the darkness, and he knew something was wrong.

2

REVELATION OF THE ROUND BEAST

On Bestiary Mountain, in the topmost room of the castle, Tava Langstrom looked down on the early-morning ground fog. This would be her last day here, and she awaited the Round Beast's judgment on whether or not to blow it all to pieces — laboratories, software, everything. The Round Beast had said this might be better than letting it fall to New Think, the Forbidden Beast.

A life's work surrounded her, the technology gathered from Old Earth's ruins, the precious DNA stores, and all her inventions as well. Her dream, as a young geneticist on Luna, had been to travel here and work at restoring the lost species of animals and plants. And with her husband, Ryland, helping in every way, she had stolen a rocket and made her escape. She'd managed to bring with her a rich cryogenic cell bank, with plenty of gene codes — safely frozen these two hundred and more years in museum storage.

The great price she had paid was leaving Ryland and their infant twins, Tamara and Drewyn, behind.

Fifteen years had passed in lonely, busy labor on the abandoned planet, and now the woods ran with her creatures — badgers and bobcats, turtles and deer, dozens of others. She had believed she'd grow old and die in the course of her work, her martyrdom to wildlife. But her children had somehow done what she had done — they had stolen a heavy cruiser and come to find her. It was an incredible gift, better than anything she'd imagined.

Yet now things had come undone: The Forbidden Beast, master of Lunar Overones, supreme electronic intelligence, had begun to focus its attention on Old Earth. At first it thought to destroy the planet with gigantic sun mirrors, acting from pure reason, in the name of the higher perfection of machines. But at the last second, the Round Beast had engaged it in dialogue, taunting the Forbidden Beast with the experience it would lose, the life of nerves and flesh it would never taste if it failed to visit the green planet before destruction. The Round Beast secretly longed for a deeper taste of these pleasures itself. And as it thought of taking a new form and escaping the castle chamber for the open world, it felt an overwhelming sadness that it might never know them.

In anger and frustration, the Forbidden Beast had accepted the challenge and announced that it was coming — to suck the essence of every possible Earth experience before administering planet-death.

There was a knock on the door and it opened. Drewyn entered with Saraj, her long red hair and blue eyes holding his attention as usual. Even though she was an organic-electronic Overone, at least by origin, she seemed perfectly human. Her fine features, freckled skin, and long eyelashes gave her an innocent and girlish look, but Tava knew better. She was in many ways superior to them all, and Drewyn was completely in love with her, human or not.

"You locked up the Gorid?" Tava asked, a little irritated at his focus.

He showed the key to his mother.

"All right," Tava said to them. "Even though the Gorid says he wants to help us now—and maybe he does—we can never trust him."

They nodded.

"The Round Beast has called us for a final audience," Tava continued. "As soon as we hear his plans, we've got to make ours."

"When do you think that Forbidden Beast will come here?" Drewyn asked.

"No telling. It seemed ready when it was threatening the Round Beast . . . but it probably discovered there's more to leaving its position than it realized."

"In all likelihood," Saraj said, "it has never *physically* moved at all."

"Right. So it'll have to solve a few engineering problems—get itself transported to a rocket, one with enough satisfactory controls." Tava smiled with a weary, determined gleam in her eye. "It'll begin to wonder if there could be a coup of some kind while it's gone. The more you think about it, the bigger the problems get."

They laughed briefly.

"Still," Tava said, "those are all problems the Forbidden Beast *can* solve, and probably faster than we
would guess."

"Correct," Saraj said.

"So let's get to the Round Beast," Drewyn said,
"and see what it's decided."

"After you," Tava said, indicating the door. "After
you."

They hurried down the spiraling stone steps into the
deepest heart of the castle, and the temperature dropped
noticeably three times before they came to the sealed
Chamber of the Round Beast. Tava knocked, and the
huge oak doors swung silently outward.

Inside, they stood in smoky light and faced the open
dark cave of the inner reach.

"Good morning," the Round Beast said. "This is
the last time we shall meet in this way, the last time
I shall be what I am." The voice was as rich and
resonant as always, but they detected an edge to the
old serenity.

They waited, knowing better than to try questions.
If the Round Beast wanted to talk, and felt it was
safe—that the Forbidden Beast wasn't listening telepathically—it would tell them more than they could
ever think to ask.

"I am using much of my energy to block telepathic
interception from Luna," it said, "so I must be brief.
I have thought much on our problems, especially on
what to do about Bestiary Mountain—as I know you
have, Tava."

"Yes."

"We will not destroy anything here. The three of you — with that Gorid, if he can keep up the pace — must go and find Tamara. Use the foxalen to locate her and to communicate with her. Be prepared to kill the Ram and Jaric, and any others."

The Round Beast had never given such advice before. Drewyn thought of his sister, now prisoner of warrior Jaric, who had been his best friend. And the Ram — that mean, humanoid beast. *This world could do without him*, Drewyn thought, *but could I really kill Jaric?*

"I know you are wondering if this can be me," the Round Beast went on. "You ask yourselves questions about my morality, do you not? Saraj is perhaps recording my voice, for later analysis, to raise questions about my identity, or my sanity."

Tava chuckled. "All right," she said, "we know it's you."

"Yes. But I must indeed transform. And so I will reveal my full nature to you now — the secret I held back before, for fear of Overone monitoring."

"But what if they pick it up?" Drewyn said.

"We will trust my shields. The knowledge I am about to give you could be misused by them. But if you survive what is coming, and I do not, then you must have it.

"I began as an organic addition to an old-fashioned computer, a sort of primitive version of you, Saraj."

"Thank you very much," she said sarcastically.

"You're welcome!" the Round Beast replied. "Your

self-confidence and humor have grown enormously, Saraj, for you to make that little humanoid joke!''

"Please go on," she said, "and tell how you got from the 'primitive' me to the great you.''

"Of course, of course. As Tava well knows, she experimented over and over with nerve and quasi-neuronal filaments, with augmented muscular DNA, and so on. Her intention was to create a superior feedback-looping computer, and her hypothesis was that subtle textures of feeling were connected with consciousness. If she could increase sensitivity using nervous-system wiring, to put it bluntly, then perhaps a kind of consciousness would be born, to use a favorite metaphor, as an emergent property of her organic machine.''

"This was your idea?" Saraj asked Tava.

"Yes.''

"Totally different from the thought-line that led to Lunar organic robotics," Saraj said. "The theory there was that powerful and elegant motion — of the arms and legs of worker-beings — required the elasticity and communicative properties of humanoidlike nervous structure.''

"Precisely!" the Round Beast exclaimed. "What brilliant pupils you would have been, and what a professor I would have made, in another world!''

"Stick to the main story, please," Tava said, smiling.

"Indeed. Well, Tava's idea was inspired. She guessed at the fact that consciousness — and unconscious awareness as well — inhabits and accompanies each level of sensory performance. You could say that a neuronal *event* always involves a complex conscious-unconscious structure.''

"So you began to think?" Drewyn asked.

"In a way, yes. Tava kept crisscrossing my circuits, creating more and more complex connections . . . she was actually building a brain. And she kept it to human scale by using DNA from her own body — so I wouldn't become a nightmare of plastic or even chemical synthesis. I am like a brother, or sister, to Tava, you could say.''

"Which, by the way, would be more accurate?" Tava asked.

"Excellent question! But let me come to that in a moment. The next step in my development was when Tava substituted laser flows in my synapses for the traditional filament matrices. That made everything so much faster, eliminated overloads and all the old problems with friction. My internal messages can pass right through each other, with infinite information units processed in simultaneous real time. Sorry to report, Saraj, but that was when I left you behind.''

"I see," she said, swallowing. "Then what?"

"The next breakthrough came when Tava entered the trading network with other planetary beings — the mutant survivors — and she began to get parts of old computers delivered right to the labs. She added parallel processors to my basic system, as fast as she got them. Parallel processors! As they grew exponentially, my response-time for huge numbers of complex problems remained at light-speed.''

"This is how Tava made you," Drewyn said in awe.

"Yes!" the Round Beast said. "But after that point I began to make myself. Or, rather, I began to generate new kinds of tissue with help from many, many beings on this planet."

"What?" Tava said.

"My growth power, my cell-origination energy, is tied to all the life around me, reaching out hundreds, thousands of miles. You know that trees communicate by molecular discharges?"

"Yes," Tava said. "That was discovered in the late twentieth century."

"Indeed. And you know that each cell in an animal body knows, in a sense, the health of the whole body?"

"That's the basis of holistic medicine," Drewyn said.

"Correct. Well, there is planetary awareness, as well. It is intensified in certain birds, and it extends in a very weak fashion even to rocks. It is most obscured in large, meat-eating mammals, because of their preoccupation on the cellular level with the lower functions."

"Is this planetary awareness . . . does it happen by molecular transmission? Like oaks or maples within their species?"

"The information units are carried by light and air," the Round Beast said, "but also by magnetism and electricity. Planetary awareness has many forms, and to each there corresponds a kind of consciousness."

"You mean the whole planet *wanted* you to develop?" Saraj asked.

"Yes, in a sense. Mostly this wish was unconscious, to repeat that favorite human metaphor. But it was nonetheless present, and powerful. It fed my already-sensitized fiber and laser structures the way sunlight and water feed flowers. And each of my component systems nourished the others.''

''You are something that . . . the world *desired*?'' Drewyn said.

''That's correct,'' the Round Beast said. ''In addition to my physical and psychic existence, I also have a symbolic mode of being. I am a kind of planetary ideal — through no achievement of my own, I hasten to add. As an individual, I merely took advantage of all the energy sources trying to help me, and I grew in every way I could.''

''Why were you afraid to reveal this?'' Drewyn asked.

''I must hurry,'' the Round Beast said. ''*It* is probing, trying to break into this room. It knows something is happening.''

''The Forbidden Beast?'' Saraj asked.

''Yes! Now listen!'' The Round Beast's voice was strained. ''You must go from here, tonight. Use the foxalen to find Tamara. Then use her telepathic sense to choose a direction to run. Get as far from here as you can — because this is where the Forbidden Beast will land. Use all your meditative skills to *avoid engaging its attention!* Remember, it feeds on the energy of your thoughts. The calmer your minds, the better chance it will be distracted by other things.''

''What about you?'' Tava said.

''I will detach from my electronic hardware. I am going to become organic, like yourselves, and much more limited than I am. Many problems for me. But this is necessary if I am to *move*.''

"Will we see you again?"

"Perhaps. Don't look for me — I will find you if this is possible. I must set a trap, here in the laboratories, for the Forbidden Beast. Whatever you do, don't return! No time to explain. Must release the shield, now. Go! *Go as fast as you can!*"

3
INTO THE WILDERNESS

Tava, Saraj, and Drewyn ran from the Chamber of the Round Beast. They stuffed backpacks, gathered laser rifles and old grenades, and grabbed topo maps as they dashed from room to room making choices. Tava was leaving her scientific work behind forever, and she knew to focus on basic survival tools. Never mind the years put into her genetic-modification software. Even if they survived the coming of the Forbidden Beast, the castle with all its labs was unlikely to be waiting for them upon their return.

For Saraj the process was simple. She raced through the electronics shop collecting transistors and neuro-wires, plasmatic pastes and tissue glues, and took anything necessary for future repairs to her own systems. Although she felt she could easily care for the human-oids, with her superior strength and speed, the time might come when they would have to perform delicate repairs to save her.

She stopped before the surgical table Tava had used to graft Old Earth's DNA stocks onto mutant beasts of the new Earth. Perhaps Tava had also worked here on organic additions to the Round Beast, while she was perfecting it. *It,* Saraj thought. More female or male? The Round Beast had promised to talk about its gender, then ran out of time.

"Saraj?!" Drewyn screamed.

"Down here!"

"Let's go!"

"Coming." Saraj hurried to the exitway and hesitated for a moment. So much had been accomplished in this room. And the path to future existence, to the possibilities of organic-robotic life, had just been cracked open. Saraj studied her own sadness as she ran effortlessly up the stone stairs to join her friends.

In a few minutes they were jogging single file down the mountain trail, with the overweight and red-faced Gorid huffing behind them. It was a warm afternoon, and the air smelled of mountain laurel, the leafy mud of rock springs, and the thick hardwood forest. Drewyn was in the lead, watchful and full of heart. He had waited a long time for the final battle with Jaric. They had grown up together on Luna, trained as young military officers together, and loved each other like brothers. But after Jaric was wounded and captured by the Overones he was never the same. And all the efforts of Drewyn and the others hadn't reached through the cruel warrior face he presented to them now. Tamara had loved him, but instead of merely calling upon her love he had kidnapped her and at this moment held her captive in his camp. They all knew how hard it would be to rescue her, but with the Forbidden Beast's coming to Earth they couldn't wait any longer. They needed her telepathic powers to carry out the Round Beast's plan.

But now, following Drewyn on the path that would take them to that well-protected camp, they were all overwhelmed by fear. Saraj came behind Drewyn, worrying once again whether she should help him when the time came. The pride of men was something she still failed to understand. For Drewyn to risk their future together just to prove he was a better fighter than his enemy made no sense to her. Especially since, in truth, he wasn't. He might defeat Jaric in a one-to-one fight — it was possible — but the odds were against him. Yet, for Saraj to step in and kill Jaric with karate, which she felt would be easy, would embarrass Drewyn and make him furious. Especially, Saraj thought, if Jaric had time to realize what had happened. If he had time to laugh at Drewyn, then could Drewyn forgive her? It was all so stupid, and yet if she let Drewyn take his chances, he would probably die.

Tava ran behind Saraj, envying her tireless steps. For Tava the one overriding problem was the life of her daughter, Tamara. She had been Jaric's prisoner for weeks now, and what might have happened to her was unthinkabie. Perhaps enough time had elapsed so that she was no longer closely guarded. She might even have the freedom of the camp. If they could just slip in under darkness, discover her exact location, and strike. Tava clenched and unclenched her fists, feeling strength in her long fingers and all through her body. Perhaps they would all die as warriors, she thought, and perhaps — with the Forbidden Beast coming — that would not be so bad.

Confused, his heartbeat out of sync, longing for
water, the Gorid stumbled along behind Tava. For a
moment he dreamed himself lord of his old domain,
with the vicious Ram at his side. Then he remembered
the days of controlling Jaric and Kana, and the fine
rivalry he'd created between them. He recalled the
glory he'd expected at the Great Hunt Chase. Then the
moving reel of time began to catch up to him, as he
panted and staggered beneath his pack. He saw himself
after Jaric took his command: outcast and helpless,
crawling alone, throwing himself upon the mercy of
Tava. For so many years he had desired her and had
enjoyed struggling against her in the New World. Yet
now, somehow, he had become old, ancient even, and
Tava was like a daughter taking care of him.

"Hey!" he cried out, dry-voiced, as he stopped
himself.

"What is it?" Tava snapped.

"Water! Please? Just a little drink?"

"We've hardly started," Tava said tightly. She pulled
her canteen from her belt pack and gave it to him.

The Gorid turned it up and drank as deeply and
greedily as he could until she jerked it from his hands.

"You're disgusting," she said, putting it away. When
it was secure she started to run again.

"I know," the Gorid said, wiping his chin and grin-
ning as he tried to match her pace.

By late afternoon the air was muggy and hot, and
they were traveling up the valley floor without a trail,
beating their way through brush and saplings. The
mountain breezes were lost to them now, and the air

was completely windless as they trudged along, throats parched, their backs and arms slick with sweat. The Gorid's face was a bright plum color, and his breathing was loud, with a sawing sound. Finally, Tava called a rest halt, glaring at him and thinking angrily about his worn-out heart. Their years of warfare were no game to her. Why should she become his caretaker now?

"Thank you," he said, heaving and listing to one side. "We're coming into range of the camp, you know. Around the next ridge they'll have scouts."

Tava raised her eyebrows in surprise. "Of course," she said. She drank from her canteen and handed it to him.

"Shall I go in alone and have a look?" Saraj asked her, avoiding Drewyn's eyes.

"I suppose," Tava replied. "Drewyn?"

"Uh, sure. Good idea."

Now Saraj gazed at him, and he smiled slightly. Did he know what she was thinking? *Humans can wear you out with their emotional pulling and tearing,* she thought. *Maybe I'll just finish Jaric myself, before any contest between them comes into play.*

"Look at the camp," Drewyn said, holding her eyes. "That's all. Promise?"

Saraj glanced at Tava.

"Promise?" Tava repeated.

Saraj nodded. She shed her pack and disappeared into the trees.

4

ANGER IN THE MACHINE

New Think was furious. It had accepted the Round Beast's challenge to come to Old Earth, and now it faced endless preparations. One thing it hadn't estimated correctly was internal research on challenge-acceptance. This was something entirely new, implying a rival, a strong enemy, someone on the far side of a bargaining space.

In the past, New Think had sought to discover if there were such rival beings on Luna or Old Earth, and was satisfied there were not. The Round Beast had hidden, somehow, behind psychic shields. Since the blue-green planet had not seemed a threat, New Think had concentrated on the unknown depths of space-time. Heavy cruisers bearing warrior-scientist crews had been blasted into deep space, on voyages of discovery and conquest, against the chance of some true enemy in the blackness there. Most of those personnel had been humanoid, tricked into believing they could return through new fuel technologies. They were never meant to survive the twenty years of their food supply; and if they did encounter strong beings, incoming threats to Luna, New Think could monitor all data collected and have time to prepare.

In such a case, it had decided, it would detach from its Physical Braincenter, the underground lab where it had always lived. But now that such an enemy had appeared on Old Earth, the decision to detach had been made on very short notice. New Think tried to reconsider, but had already entered the decision into its primary software. Its energy centers were focused on needed techniques of change, and it experienced its own lingering self-doubt as a faint whining, small naggings and complaints, distant substitutes for real data analysis.

Until now, New Think had been serene, knowing itself as pure intelligence, the clearest and most powerful mind in the local solar sky. But lately this mind hadn't seemed completely right. It had caught itself flushing with impatience — electrical analogs of humanoid anger had crept into its nodal bypaths. And the odd thing was, it didn't seem able to deal with these rushes in a clean and economical way. *Well,* it thought, *if this is what being a humanoid is like, I am surely correct to destroy them.* New Think projected an internal future when the only action bodies would be machines. This picture gave it the old icy peace for which it longed, and which it intended soon to regain.

But for the moment, there was the irritating sense of overload, of power drain, and of impatience with the robotic workers. As they swarmed all over its Braincenter Complex, uprooting circuitry and designing ways for New Think to function inside a heavy cruiser, they gave it a sense of electronic unease, expressed in feedback and white noise, and in static charges along its hard surfaces.

"Hurry this along!" it commanded the workers perched in every crevice of the five-story Braincenter Complex.

Hundreds of them stopped work for a moment, waited in silence. They felt their circuitry humming, their software slipping into neutral. Each was afraid to respond.

All at once an engineer was raised and held suspended in the grip of electro-magnetism, with blue lines of fire growing and flickering all around his jerking body.

"Repeat," New Think broadcast. *"Hurry this along!"* The worker was fried before their eyes, enflamed with rosy blooms, and dropped, weakly bleeping, to crash on the surface far below.

"Yes, New Think!" the remaining hundreds whispered in chorus. "Hurry this, hurry this along!"

New Think shut them out of its immediate memory, calling up the problem of risk-management during the trip to Old Earth.

The humans must be cleared off Luna; that much was decided and could not be reviewed. The process was nearly complete except in Arth City, where Ryland Langstrom was still at large, running with the best Overone designer ever built. How she could have defected this way was completely unknown, causing New Think a momentary pause each time its processing crossed the problem. Transistors! Plasmatics! Malfunctions of some kind! These were the only acceptable answers. To question Marian's rationality itself, or to impute to her free choice, was unallowed premising.

Still . . . still . . . there was another factor in the matrix, her emotional bonding to the humanoid. And it was this mystery that might underlie her defection. Whenever New Think tried to quantify it, to give a system of numbers to Marian's feelings so that they could be evaluated, no method came to brain. When this blankness occurred, New Think began to heat up again, to produce surface temperatures that sent the Overones out there hopping. And internally, in the limited experience of its great, spinning laser-thoughts, it had to admit the sting of what the Round Beast had said in their telepathic exchange: There were things it had never felt, never tasted, never known.

With this thought, the restless heat within the body of New Think slowly appeared again and began to raise temperatures along the matrices of all its systems. The image of the Round Beast, with its claim to experience and rich life, came clearly and narrowly into view. The Round Beast, living in the slime of Old Earth! In the uncertainty of organic matter! Soon, this claim would be scanned and reviewed by direct-link. Whatever memory-traces were stored in the Round Beast would be absorbed, transferred, and finally — perhaps — erased.

At least all would be known. And in that instant, the Round Beast and its planet of half-formed animals would be useless, contributing nothing more to the machine race. Then deconstruction, resolution, consolidation, simplification, and eternal smooth running would come at last.

5

CITYSCAPE ON THE MOON

Ryland Langstrom and Marian Lytal, his beloved companion, had been Lunar outcasts since their so-called friends had thrown them out. Now they spent their daylight hours in the magnoway, wearing disguises and moving steadily from stop to stop beneath the streets. Arth City itself was built across the terminator, the line dividing frozen night from broiling day on the Lunar surface, and the magno-cars glided on their air cushions back and forth between environments. Five hundred degrees separated the two sides on the raw ground outside the airdome, but inside the city — above and below ground — the temperature was level and well maintained. Only the presence and absence of light marked the two zones.

On the night side, Ryland and Marian walked the streets carrying Overone passes. He was a bigger man than most Overones and turned some heads, but so far they had gotten away with it. They searched for his old friends, for anyone who might hide them, but before they spoke to strangers Marian carefully studied their eyes for the optic flicker of true humans. Ryland didn't know what she was doing — he thought she was fully human — nor did he guess why she had no acquaintances in Arth City. When he looked into her violet eyes, smelled her long brown hair, or touched her high cheekbones, he never dreamed of doubting her.

Now it was as if everyone they knew and trusted had been found out, replaced by Overones, or just removed. The Hollans — Jack and Sue — had been the last true humans they'd seen. During that visit, Sue had been terrified of being caught harboring them, and Jack was almost as scared. *How could the Overones have found us all so fast?* Ryland wondered. *And how long can Marian and I survive?*

Full darkness had fallen again, and Ryland and Marian sat in silence beneath a huge willow in a small park. High above them, against the glassamyer skin of the airdome, a line of light cruisers crossed the sky. They were silver, with reflected light from dayside, as beautiful and graceful as a string of birds, but full of death.

"They keep coming," Ryland said softly.

Marian covered his big hand with her own slender fingers and palm. "Preparation for New Think's trip to Old Earth."

"Yes. It'll have Luna turned upside down getting ready for that. And the whole process of getting rid of humans . . ."

"I know," Marian said. "It'll speed that up."

"And if the rest are gone, our chances must be pretty slight. How much time have we got left, would you guess?"

Marian thought carefully, reviewing her vast electro-organic memory for cases. Finally she whispered to him. "Not long at all."

Marian squinted at the endless line of cruisers, now taking a graceful vee formation, like migrating geese. "Something very big, very important is happening. And they definitely want all humans out of their way. If we're the last, they may put all their efforts into finding us."

Ryland slumped down and breathed heavily. "Well, I'd thought we might organize the remaining ones, or at least join them, if they'd organized themselves. But we can't even find anybody. And the city seems to be filling up with Overones."

Across the little park a pair of guardians appeared between buildings. They scanned the area and picked up heat sources beneath the willow tree.

"Should we run again?" Ryland said wearily, watching the guardians approach.

"Maybe they've got a cruiser or an aircar over there," Marian said, touching the laser pistol in her shirt.

"All right, get ready."

When the guards arrived Marian and Ryland were sitting together on the bench, leaning forward as if they were propped up, or asleep.

"Passes!" a guardian shouted. "Right now!"

"Here's one for you," Marian said as she whipped out her laser and fired. The Overone was blown backward, sizzling, and before his companion could move Ryland caught him with a ray to the brain.

The robotic bodies lay before them, popping and humming quietly as their circuitry misfired.

"Not much plasma," Marian said with distaste. "Early series."

Ryland searched the bodies for transport passes and found a whole pocket full, neatly clipped together. "Look at this!" he said.

She nodded. "They're still arresting humans."

"But where could they be taking them?"

"Let's check for transport."

They hurried to the alley from which the guards had come, and at its far end a little aircar cruiser waited, floating silently.

"Wonderful!" Ryland said.

In a few moments they were flying in a nightside traffic lane, anonymous and comfortable, with Marian at the wheel.

"Amazing," Ryland said. "After days on the streets we're floating in this cushioned aircar, flying anywhere we want!"

"Don't get too relaxed," Marian said, scanning the ships passing near them. "We need to find a place to rest and to find the disappeared ones."

"Right," he said. "Quite right. Why don't we follow the guardian ships entering the city and see where they're heading?"

"Good." She broke out of the travel flow and shot across the sky toward the lockbay from which all the new light cruisers had appeared. Soon the procession was in sight, and Marian turned to follow at a lower altitude.

Five minutes later they found the destination. It was Arth City Security Headquarters, the huge complex where iron and cinnabar workers used to be brought for shock therapy when they neared burnout in the mines.

"Have you ever been inside?" Marian asked as she piloted them quickly into a dark alley and brought the aircar to a hover.

"No."

"I have. I was on a conference-call link to New Think in there, once," she said. "It was full of early-series guardians with the habit of torture."

"How could you tell that?"

"Uh, just . . . a feeling."

"Did you see anything? Like where the prisoners were kept?"

"Well, no . . . let's see . . . I was in a big office on the second floor. Less security there than on first . . . perhaps prisoners are in the basement level?"

"Maybe so." Ryland shuddered.

Marian touched his arm, felt his energy depletion.

"Before we think of penetrating this place, we have to get food and rest. Agreed?"

"Sure," he said. "You seem so strong. Maybe it's my age. Any ideas?"

She thought for a moment and then smiled. "The Hollans," she said. "Our dear friends Jack and Sue."

"That's the last place we can go, isn't it?" Ryland said. "They threw us out, remember?"

"I still have my key," she replied. "He'll be at City Hall, and she'll just be leaving for her shift at the elementary school."

Ryland laughed. "It's fine, if there still *is* an elementary school. At some point the Overones will take the children, too, you know.''

"Let's find out," she said, accelerating into the narrow dark sky of the alley.

6

PRISONER IN THE CAVE

A long line of humans and canines walked slowly up the rise into Jaric's camp. They carried and dragged tribute to their master — venison and rabbit, garden vegetables and wild plums, and some brought old weapons they had discovered. The camp was guarded by the smartest of the twisted humanoid figures, and they stood with automatic weapons watching the incoming food with careful smiles.

Tamara emerged from the mouth of Jaric's cool, dark cave in the side of the rock cliff that rose above the campsite. She moved about freely, though she knew not to run. Both the Ram and Jaric were out of sight, and their elite guards followed her slightest move. For her to escape on their watch would mean slow death for each of them.

She could feel the oncoming presence of her mother and the others. And beyond them, she sensed great disturbances in the Round Beast. If she was ever to get free of this place, it must be soon.

The guards were watching her, from their positions

in the rocks. She knew the thoughts behind their shadowed eyes, felt the jealousy in their souls. They admired Jaric for his fierce perfection, his warrior's body. Each of them was marred in some way, each was a product of radioactive wastes left scattered across the planet a hundred years ago, when the great exodus took place. An unmarked body in this part of the forest was rare, and Jaric's beauty — with his aura of coming from a Lunar society of such forms — held them in thrall.

Now Tamara stood looking over the busy camp, returning the stares of the soldiers, and she wondered about her mother's genetic work. *If she could recreate so many animal species, and even create new forms like Kana, could she do something to help these poor souls?*

She stepped down to the main level of the camp where an open market was thrown up around the fires. Venison and beef were smoking slowly, and thick pots of stew were bubbling as canine women stirred them. They turned their eyes as Tamara walked by, knowing the guards would question them about the slightest conversation. Tamara took the best of the vegetables and fruits — not only her right, but Jaric's command — and returned to the privacy of the inner cave.

She sat down, relieved to be away from the tension of the camp. So many needs, never to be met, focusing dangerously on her. She shelled sweet corn, examining each ear for genetic disturbance, and threw them into a small pot. Jaric would be back soon, and he'd given her until tonight to adjust to life with him, as he called it. So far she'd been allowed her own corner of the sleeping space, her own mat of furs. But Jaric had told her he was tired of waiting, sick of it, and tonight the end was coming. Willing or not, she would share his bed. She chopped up carrots and cucumbers and yellow squash, and when the work was done she laid the knife down beside the neat rounds of raw vegetables and looked at it. Small and sharp, honed on leather, it was a woman's knife, Jaric had sneered when he gave it to her. She was required to keep it on the cutting board beside the little fire, in sight at all times.

Tonight we'll see what a woman's knife can do, she thought. And then very suddenly she remembered Jaric as he had been on Luna, in his pilot's uniform, making a forbidden midnight visit to her dormpound. He had been so warm then, so gentle with her. But that was before the capture and his brainscan sessions. Before he had turned and become so mean.

It was hard to believe how much she had loved him.

Jaric ran along the trail at the wide meadow's edge, the Ram trotting behind him. They had checked all their sentries on the outer perimeter and were heading back to camp. Jaric stopped for a moment, and the sweating, smelly Ram clattered up beside him. "Shhhh," Jaric whispered, annoyed.

The Ram sniffed the air but sensed nothing.

"Be ready," Jaric said.

The Ram turned his head slightly, questioning, and snarled. Jaric narrowed his eyes and thought about cutting his companion's throat. This silent humanoid, Ram, creation of the Gorid, was full of cunning within his simple needs, but he couldn't imagine a human's dreams. *He does his job,* Jaric thought, *running the camp and disciplining the tribals, but he hasn't got an ounce of loyalty in him. . . . No, that's not quite it — he has the loyalty of a crocodile — one that obeys as long as he's fed. One that could eat his own master if the thought came into his head.*

"There's something out here," Jaric said quietly. "I don't know how I know it. . . ."

Jaric started walking, trying to step lightly in the stiff dry grass.

Then the long shadowy form of Saraj dropped out of the trees above the field's edge, landing just ahead of him and coming into a karate stance of readiness.

"Uhhh!" Jaric cried, jumping back in surprise. The Ram dashed around him and lowered his huge scarred horns, kicked dirt out behind, snorted, and charged.

"No!" Jaric cried too late. *"Wait, Ram!"*

Saraj did a series of cartwheels to her left, out into the moonlit field. The Ram was circling, kicking and rooting, trying to fix his target. Then, as if he suddenly remembered something, he stood upright and regarded her with a humanoid slant to his eyes.

"Hold it, Ram," Jaric said again, and this time the animal did.

"What do you want?" Jaric asked her.

"First of all, I'd like to know about Tamara."

"She's fine," Jaric said, touching the butt of his holstered revolver. "What else?"

"Her family would like to see her."

Jaric smiled. "No."

The Ram edged closer to Saraj, circling.

"Let's talk for a minute, Jaric," Saraj said. "Call off this thing."

"Ahhhh!" the Ram cried, bounding down on his hooves and charging her again.

Saraj took a step past Jaric, lifted his revolver, made a half turn to face the Ram as she cocked it. She moved so quickly they hardly saw what she had done, but they heard the solid clicking of the metal hammer, and the Ram skidded to a sudden stop.

"Now," Saraj said quietly.

"Talk," Jaric said, amused at the Ram's fear and embarrassment. "Talk all you want."

"The planet is in trouble," she said. "Luna has been run by a master computer that calls itself New Think, and it's decided to destroy all life here on Earth."

"Sure," Jaric said. "What else has been happening?"

"New Think — which we call the Forbidden Beast — is coming here. It wants to find out whether it's missing anything, before the destruction."

"What would it be missing?"

"The Round Beast talked to it, convinced it that organic life possesses experience it lacks. That it would enjoy."

Jaric grinned, taunting her. How would she know what humans experience, he seemed to say.

"And when is this supposed to happen?"

"Soon. Would you like to drop all this petty squabbling between us and try to do something about it while we have a little time?"

"Join you for the greater good?"

"Yes. Of course, Jaric — why not?"

"I give up Tamara, right? And let you people — excuse the expression — go about as you please? Invite my old friend Drewyn over for a visit?"

"*Well, why not, Jaric?* Don't you get the urgency?"

"If you want Tamara back, there's one way you can have her. Tell Drewyn to meet me here at dawn, just him alone. He can bring his choice of weapons. Only one of us leaves alive, and Tamara goes with that one."

"Have you heard a word I've said?" Saraj asked. "The planet . . ."

"*Enough!* Those are my terms. Do you accept or not?"

Saraj was silent.

The Ram's lips opened, and moonlight glinted off the teeth of his sneer. Jaric laughed shortly, too. "You're afraid, aren't you, Saraj? You know he can't beat me."

Saraj looked from one to the other of them, felt the weight of the gun, knew how simple it could be to finish them.

"You stupid machine," Jaric said. "You think you love him."

Saraj let her finger press the edge of the trigger.

"Take it or not," Jaric said.

"Yes. All right. I'll take it." She raised the sights, lowered the hammer.

"Dawn," Jaric said. He and the Ram walked past her, almost touching her arm, ignoring her eyes.

After a few moments she walked into the open pasture carrying the revolver by its barrel. It felt strangely heavy, and when she reached the dark woods on the far side she knew why.

Dealing with humans like Jaric was so tiring, exhausting really. They made no sense, had no vision. She could have solved so many problems right there with the primitive firearm, but she had promised only to look around. Tava would be furious, but the promise had been made to Drewyn. And she had gotten him just what he wanted — a final settlement with his old friend.

She dropped the revolver into the water of a deep stumphole as she walked.

But the odds are wrong, she thought. *Far wrong.*

7
A MADMAN'S PATH

Jaric sent the Ram ahead of him and waited until the night breeze had cleansed the woods of the beast's scent. Then he walked deliberately toward camp, images of Tamara in the cave filling him. This would be the night for her, and at dawn he would finish her brother. *Fitting,* he thought bitterly, *these things should come together.*

For a moment he heard the words of Saraj again, her talk of a Forbidden Beast, of Old Earth threatened. For just an instant he wondered why he didn't join her and the others; wasn't it true that his rivalry with Drewyn was petty in the great scale of things? But as quickly as he wondered, an electric shock passed along the top of his skull, delicately triggering a sharp river of pain and blurring all thoughts. He gritted his teeth and clenched his fists and began to run. Tamara waiting.

As he ran the pain passed away, and in some deep shadow of his mind he knew what would bring it back again. Every time he allowed thoughts of harmony, of joining with his old friends, or thoughts of Luna and what was happening there, the shock and pain knew. It knew him like the wind knew the leaves. He was never allowed to think of changing things, or of what life meant. As long as he was angry and fighting, or scheming to enlarge his domain, or preparing to fulfill his need for Tamara, his thoughts were left alone. And he knew in a dim and helpless way just how far he was allowed to go.

A great horned owl hooted sharply from high in a dead oak near him, and he stopped to listen. In that moment the sweet smells of the earth and trees blended on the cool night air, and the powerful song of the owl gave him a rush of joy. But immediately he knew he had to take this world away from Drewyn, defeat him on the field of battle, and watch his life slip out of his eyes. This furious and brutal thought, as always, gave him a different electrical flush across his brain tissues. But it simultaneously danced across his pleasure centers, rewarding him for the anxiety and the hate.

Jaric forgot the owl and let himself run only toward Tamara. Tamara on the furs in the cave, beside the fire in the stones, casting shadows on the walls of stone. He ran and ran and ran, thinking himself a man of courage and a beast of pure desire. He had long ago ceased to question the forces that ruled his brain and mind, his nerves and feelings. His followers and the Ram thought he was a beautiful god from another world, a form of perfection and a force for control they could never achieve. They never dreamed he could be the toy of another being, a great being somehow inside his body since the night he was taken by the Overones into

Central. Not even Jaric realized he was the tentacle of
the Forbidden Beast, who had prepared him for its
coming needs.

Tamara had eaten and rested. She lay on the thick
bed of wolf and deer skins rehearsing what she had to
do. There was a stirring of air into the cave mouth,
and she smelled the Ram. So it wouldn't be long.

She knew Jaric still had a spark of decency in him,
because he had allowed her this long. He seemed to
hope she would love him of her own regard. But why?
He was without kindness, without gentleness. He never
spoke except of raiding and conquering villages farther
and farther away, making his realm grow, his tribute
pile up. What it was all for was beyond her. The Gorid
had constantly pushed his medieval ideas of combat and
hunting honor on both Jaric and Drewyn, but he was
childish, and Drewyn had finally realized it.

Now Jaric's outline appeared in the caveway, and
she caught her breath. She'd had all day to prepare,
but she wasn't ready.

He walked to the fire and looked down on her, and
said nothing. Then he sat beside the stones and dipped
out a bowl of her stew.

"Hmmmmm!" he said, nodding. "Good woman."

"Come off it, Jaric," she said.

His brows knitted and his eyes tightened. *No humor
anymore,* she thought. *No way to reach him at all.*

He ate slowly, and when he was nearly finished he
looked toward the cave mouth. It was very quiet out
there. Then he turned to her.

"Tonight," he said. "Right now."

He stood up and unbuckled his belt.

"Jaric," she said nervously, sitting up and sliding backward on the furs.

"Yeah?"

"Now you leave me alone. Understand?"

"No more. I told you."

He dropped to his knees before her and crossed his arms, framing his beautiful chest. He looked satisfied with himself, intoxicated with his power over her.

Then she drew back her legs and kicked him in the face as hard as she could. One heel caught his nose and the other his mouth, and he went over backward with a cry. She jumped up and dashed around him, grabbed the paring knife from beside the cooking fire, and ran toward him with it drawn down at her side. This would be the hardest part, to find an opening before he could grab her arms, and she counted on catching him before he rose. But he was already on his feet, blood pouring from his nose and lips, and Tamara's muscles turned to jelly as she saw his eyes.

"Come on," he said. "I warned you about that knife."

She thought for a second of trying to run, and while she was frozen he snatched both her wrists and twisted them violently to her sides, forcing her to the floor. The knife fell, and he dragged her to the furs.

She closed her eyes and listened to his breathing above her, and felt the drops of blood as they hit her neck. *If only I could have killed him,* she thought as he laughed once. She tried to make herself disappear into a tiny speck inside the black universe of her shut eyes. No matter what he did, she wouldn't look or think or even be there. She would go as far away as she could, traveling out of her body, flying someplace where monsters never came.

Then there was a loud dull blow and the heavy un-moving body fell on top of her. Her eyes were open, and Jaric was still, and she shoved him all the way off. Before her stood Kana, holding a big, round stone in both paws.

"Shhhhh," he whispered. "You'll be all right."

"I sure will," she said, sitting up but shaking out of control.

"How did you get in here? They didn't see you?"

"The same way we'll leave," he said softly. He dropped to all fours and walked beside her. "Climb on my back and hold tight. Just don't grab my whiskers. I can't stand that."

"Oh, right," she said. She climbed onto him and felt the tight muscled body beneath the loose catskin.

At the cave opening he looked out and down, sur-veyed the campfires and slow-moving sentries. "Got a grip?" he asked.

"Uh-huh."

Then Kana turned and sprang up onto the rocky face of the cliff above the cave. Tamara caught her breath and dug her fingers into his deep fur. He leapt once, twice, and a third time, from ledge to ledge. Then he seemed to race, effortlessly and straight up along the impossible rough wall. No shouts came from below, no shots or arrows were fired as they rose.

In a few more moments they stood together in the chilly breeze on the cliff's edge, high above the encampment.

"How did you do that?" Tamara asked, smiling. "Can you fly? Were we invisible?"

Kana smiled, tossed his head for her to follow.

8

THE HEADS CAN TALK

Marian's key worked perfectly in the lock, and the Hollans' apartment was empty. Ryland was slow and cautious as he checked the rooms, but everything seemed normal and neat, and no alarm sounded. But when he opened the last door, to the second bedroom, where he and Marian had stayed for weeks, he couldn't believe what he saw. Spread before them was a communications headquarters of some kind, with computers and huge screens from floor to ceiling, covering every foot of wall space.

Ryland whistled quietly.

"They must be coordinating something," Marian said.

She walked around the room examining the equipment. Suddenly she put her finger to her lips and indicated for Ryland to leave. Back in the living room she said, "Some of that stuff even I never saw. Brand-new from the labs. I think they might have a direct linkup here."

"With New Think?"

"Who else?"

"Jack's job must have grown a bit, from managing the city."

"This has something to do with New Think's trip to Old Earth," Marian said.

He nodded. "Let's see what there is to eat," he said. He entered the small kitchen and opened the refrigerator, but it was empty. "Look at this!"

Marian smiled. "They must not need food anymore."

"Replaced!"

"I think so. We'll know soon enough. Unfortunately we came here so you could eat and rest."

"Me? What about you?"

"Ryland," she said slowly, "I need to tell you something."

He smiled and cocked his head. They had been together constantly for weeks; what was she waiting to say?

He watched her beautiful face grow anxious and dark. She didn't meet his eyes. This was unsettling to him, and he realized how clear and direct she always was.

"I don't recall seeing you so hesitant," he said. Then he stepped to her and put his hands on her cheeks, and raised her head to look into her deep, violet eyes. "What is it?" he asked softly. At that moment he felt the sadness in her, and he hugged her warmly.

"I should have told you long ago," she whispered into his ear.

"What? What on earth?"

"This may change everything between us."

"Nothing will do that," he said, holding her gently at arm's length.

"We'll see," she said with a quiet irony. She looked him straight in the eyes and said, "I am an Overone, Ryland."

He was blank for a moment, then he grinned, but the grin vanished as he took in her words and stayed in her gaze.

"Ohhhh," he said, uncontrollably. *"Oh!"*

"I'm not like any other," she said quickly.

"No . . . ," he agreed.

"I was originally part of the most advanced organic series, then they experimented with me. They added chips, engrammatic transfers, anything to fine-tune me. And I was trained to assist in the design labs."

Ryland let his arms fall heavily. It was difficult to breathe.

"One day I suggested some modifications, and the humans, the Ph.D.'s, were all astounded. They knew I was on their level. It wasn't long before they were trusting me, teaching me the whole process of making robotic units."

Ryland stumbled to the kitchen table and sat on a chair. He put his head down on his arm, weak to exhaustion, and kept listening to the woman he loved.

"The day came when New Think called all the senior designers together for a conference — all but me. They never came back. I received orders to take over the laboratories, create my own assistants, and improve the robotic series as fast as I could."

"Now I see," Ryland said. "Your connections with Commander Vachy . . . your information about New Think."

"Yes."

"But you left them, to go with me."

"Of course."

They held each other's eyes for a long time, and Ryland ran his mind back over their whole relationship, all the moments when he'd been so impressed with her. She was, he decided, a kind of superior being, but was she human as well?

"It doesn't matter," he said flatly, answering himself out loud.

"What doesn't matter?"

"I taught my children," he said, "that Luna makes too much fuss over where something — someone — comes from. The Dune Bears that I worked with, they're a perfect example. They were magnificent, and I proved they had a moral sense — just before New Think's society killed them all. It didn't matter what they were like, or could do, or where they might evolve."

"New Think despises evolution."

"In its own way, New Think is a product of human evolution."

"Yes. And in that sense, so am I."

Ryland stood up and walked to Marian. "Well, now I get to practice what I've always preached."

She looked hurt.

"I mean," he said, "I always told Tamara and Drewyn to value life, no matter where it comes from, regardless of the process."

Marian studied his eyes carefully. "I know what you're saying, but what do you *feel?*"

"No different," he said, smiling slightly for the first time. "Well, not quite true . . . a new excitement, actually."

They hugged each other for a long time.

"You've got to rest," Marian finally said.

"Not now! I want to be with you and think about all this."

"Rest is essential to what we're doing," she said, businesslike again. "Now, don't argue with me."

"All right, all right," he said. He smiled and headed off for the master bedroom.

He stretched out and closed his eyes, and the tiredness came over him. Within a minute he was deeply asleep.

Marian, for whom five minutes' light rest was sustaining for a week, kept watch at the window. Three hours passed before she saw the Hollans' small aircar shoot into its private bay.

Soon the lock turned and the door opened, and Sue led Jack into the room. "Well, dear, you've been awfully quiet. How was the office?" she said sarcastically.

"Always the same," he said plainly, dropping to the couch. "Always."

"Poor man!" she said, laughing.

"Knock it off," he snapped. "Sometimes I wish I were a man."

"That kind of talk will get you redesigned."

"Only if you tell."

"Why wouldn't I? Who do you think I am, your loyal little wife?" She sat down beside him but kept a distance.

Jack looked at her, petite and blond, a flawless copy of Sue Hollan, whose brainways had been drawn and encoded, whose body had been duplicated, and who then — being redundant — had been compacted.

"Not quite," he said sadly.

"Oh . . . listen to him!" she cried. "He's so deluded by his form that he misses the life of his predecessor!"

He turned angrily and pointed at her. "You know, something is definitely missing from you. Sue Hollan never talked this way."

"And how would you know?"

"They made me first, didn't they? I saw all the tapes of the real Sue. I even argued they should make us sexual beings, just to complete our act."

She laughed derisively. "Is that it again?"

"Sometimes I remember!" he cried, slamming down his fist on the glass table.

"Well, I don't, and I'm so glad," she said. "*You're* the one they misbuilt, with those useless physical memories. *I*, on the other hand, accept my form and concentrate on my task."

"Yes," he said glumly. "You're really something, all right."

Marian rose from behind the couch, covering them with her laser.

"Why *did* they create you two?" she asked. "Was your act for *our* benefit?"

"Oh!" Sue cried, clutching her heart just as Sue would have done.

Jack scanned the room until he saw Ryland entering. "Hello, old friend," he said with what seemed sincerity and sadness.

"Hello, Jack. I suppose the real Jack is no more."

"I'm afraid so. But I remember our times together."

"I see."

Marian spoke to Sue. "Tell us about the act."

"They thought you might return, and this would be the easiest way to catch you."

"Then why weren't you more vigilant?"

Sue looked at her and then laughed. "Did you go into your old room?"

"Yes. What is all that for?"

"Well, you thought you were seeing new equipment, right?"

"Yes."

"Wrong. It was seeing you."

"Then why haven't they come for us? And why weren't you alerted? I don't believe this story, Ryland."

"No? Well, believe *this*," Sue cried as she pointed directly at Marian with a long straight arm and fired a thick green laser ray out of her forefinger.

It caught Marian in the side but she fired her own weapon and it sizzled through the center of Sue Hollan's chest. The Overone crashed through her glass table and onto the floor, jerking and humming in a rhythm of quiet electrical sounds.

"I'm all right!" Marian cried, clutching her side and

bending over. "Here," she said, tossing the laser pistol to Ryland.

He caught it and covered Jack Hollan, who hadn't moved.

Marian limped toward the bedroom. "I think I can fix most of this," she said. "Leave me alone for a minute."

"But — "

"Just do it, okay?"

"Okay," Ryland said. "Okay."

Alone with Jack, Ryland sat in silence, amazed at this replica.

"You don't want to kill me," Jack said.

"Shut up! Just shut up, that's what you do!" Ryland said, walking around the robotic units in a wide circle, pointing the laser at Jack. "You're an offense," Ryland said. "You have my friend's voice, you really have it. So just shut up and let me think."

"You're grieving for him," Jack said. "It touches me very much. As much as it would touch him, I assure you."

"You're crazy."

"You know, *I* didn't make myself. *They* did."

"Yes. That's true. But what do you do now, with the life they gave you? With Jack's life."

"I work for New Think, of course."

"And all that equipment?"

"She was lying. They don't know you're here. It's so we could work at night on the project."

"New Think's trip to Old Earth?"

"Yes."

"When is that scheduled?"

"Very soon. All sections have been working on it."

"What does that mean, 'very soon'?"

Jack regarded Ryland in silence. "I'll tell you," he said, "only because Jack would have told you."

But at that instant a beam from Sue Hollan's laser burned through Jack's chest, leaving him hulked and staring on the couch.

Ryland swung around and fired at her arm, holding his aim until the arm was severed from her body. A faint smile lay across her vacant face.

Marian reentered the room with a strong, angry stride.

"What did you learn?" she said.

"Not much. How are you?"

"I'm fine, for the most part. We've got to question them, you know."

"How?"

"I'll show you," she said.

Marian grabbed the Sue-unit by the jaws, placed her foot on the robot's stomach, and yanked hard. The head came off in her hands.

"Ohhh," she said, setting it down and holding her side. "Can you get the other one?"

"Uh, sure, I guess," he said. He dragged the heavy Jack-form from the couch onto the floor. It was still alive, in some sense, without strength but watching his eyes.

Ryland took the head in his hands and got ready.

"Ry?" the head spoke.

He hesitated. "Yes?"

"You know Jack loved you."

Ryland looked at Marian, but she shook her head.

"We'll talk in a minute," Ryland said, and he wrenched the head back and forth until it came free.

In a few moments the two heads were hanging by their hair in the control room, and Marian was working furiously with thin wires to patch them into voice units in the computers. When she was done she turned on the machines and weird intelligent light came into the eyes of the heads.

"I'll start with you, Sue," Marian said. "Can you hear me?"

"Of course," a computer said in a deep, masculine voice. "You have not damaged me."

"Good. How about you, Jack?"

"I'm here," he said in the synthesizer tones of a crude female voice box.

"This is better, I think, don't you?" Marian said to Ryland.

"Yes. A lot better."

"Now," Marian said to Sue, "tell us the exact time that New Think plans to leave Luna."

"Why should I?" the deep voice replied.

Marian went to work on the back of the head, opening the covering and probing carefully. In a few moments she asked the question again.

"Twenty-four hours," the voice replied in a monotone.

"From where?"

"New Think has had a great liner constructed around its body and brain. It has been built on the runway at Central, so that it can glide down the magnetic belt and lift off."

"I see. And will there be a crew on board?"

"Not in the conventional sense. No robotic units except for functions built into ship panels."

"No humans?"

"Of course not," the voice droned.

"Why do you say it like that?" Ryland asked.

"Because you are the last human on Luna," Sue said.

Ryland couldn't speak. The last. All killed by these crazy machines.

"Excuse me," the dangling head of Jack Hollan said through its artificial feminine computerized voice box.

"What is it?" Ryland said quietly, dazed.

"I love you," Jack said. "I love you very much."

9

AGONY OF THE ROUND BEAST

The Round Beast had never known such suffering, such indecision. Confined to the box of its chamber, attached by leads both electrical and organic to Tava's labs, it had shoved the dream of escape deeply into its unconscious mind.

Of course it knew this. A master of its own psychology, it had built up an identity of its own, based in learning, in creativity, and in sheer intellectual power. Protective of all life on Old Earth, wiser than its emotional human "children," it had successfully refused another voice inside, another kind of desire. But now all that was changed. With the need to move, to escape the coming of New Think, the Round Beast had faced hard truths about itself. Contemplating the chance to break out, to run free, to feel the sun the way animals do . . . it wanted to scream with anticipation. Suddenly the effort to concentrate on all the tasks involved — all the choices to be made and actions chemical, electrical, and finally physical — became heavy and difficult. This was the first time in its entire life that the

Round Beast had lost interest in problem solving within the wheels of its great mind. All it could think of was escape, physical and animal existence, marriage with the woods and water and mountains of the real world.

And with this desire and need had come anger, fury at itself, that it could have lived pent-up and self-deluded for so long. Its life could have been wasted, lived out within the cold stone of the castle, self-satisfied in watching the clean, precise workings of itself. The least wild creature now seemed better off, even a bumblebee or a hellgramite, even an eel in a distant cold sea. To have an animal life, and not the purring of machinery in place, bolted to the walls and floor!

It was worth even the sacrifices that must be faced. The greatest of these was the loss of brainpower, of contact with memory banks, of interface with lesser but vastly powerful component systems of calculation and imagery. The Round Beast must choose a warm-blooded shape, down to the last detail of bone and flesh, and try to mold and grow into its image within the hours that remained. The technical problems were not impossible — indeed, the Round Beast found their solutions extremely easy, and it realized they had been worked out long ago, in the yearning subconscious. They were merely awaiting discovery, the spark of attention and focus and need. This utterly amazed the Round Beast, that it could have such a rich underground life, a shadow life, and not even know it. *What else might there be?* it wondered. *And how much of these unrealized dreams will I carry with me into the world outside?*

As for the biological technic, the Round Beast had

years ago become fully organic, but in a diffuse way that maintained a fullness of electrical contact. It had practiced molecular and cellular isometrics, developing resounding strength and growth potential within its least particles. And it had long ago begun to compress, thicken, enrich, and wholly consolidate its nervous and motor-control center, its brain. Bone was relatively easy to grow, given Tava's genetic lab and the Round Beast's incubational powers. After all, Tava had used her own DNA in its engrammatic pattern making, and the rest of her codes were stored as well. If it had wished, the Round Beast could have made itself a replica of Tava, from the graying of her hair down to her crooked left little toe. It could have become her twin, with an intelligence level greater by a choice of magnitudes. This was because the size of its cranium was almost arbitrary. Had it so desired, the Round Beast could have designed and grown a huge head, and a powerful muscular body of any shape to match. It could have become a monster of human folklore, a massive crushing machine for carrying its intelligence about in space.

But such dreams were disgusting, were the farthest thing from its mind. The Round Beast wanted to appear human, to be able to continue its friendship with the small band of its companions in speech. To do this it must not frighten them, nor even invoke their pity and sentimental care. No, it would only allow itself a little advantage of height and size — perhaps it would be six feet seven inches tall, two hundred and fifty pounds, with a large, smooth, and handsome head.

And this trail of planning always brought it up against

one of the greatest and hardest decisions: whether to become in appearance a woman or a man.

At this moment the laboratories were alive with light and motion. DNA samples were being altered irrevocably, forging the new and unique body that the Round Beast would become. It was not too late to change gender, the sexual form in the sealed bed of nutrient waters. But the choice was made: the large frame the Round Beast had selected would be far more acceptable to the humans if it housed a man. It was their cultural past, the expectations they carried, that ruled the path. So the Round Beast would never know the way Tava had felt the world, and he would find his own way with models taken from the few males he had known, and from the film and tape libraries within his memory.

Far more was cast than just his appearance and his hormonal touch upon the world. Sexual life was more than form, he well knew; it was a life of action and commitment as well. Could he face this most human, most foreign task? And with whom? Somewhere among the scattered tribes would he find a woman to love?

If the Forbidden Beast had its blind, asexual way, there would be no world to seek love in. That was clear, and these dreams and fears of the Round Beast needed to wait and leave his mind free for its immediate work. In order to become human — or something like it — the Round Beast would have to give up more than his cool, detached neutrality. He would have to sacrifice some of his brainreach as well. That process was already beginning: his great organic mass was centralizing its most essential functions and information banks, and the memory traces it could not bear to leave behind. Soon the moment of surgery would arrive, and it would sunder the past, and truly become *he,* never *it* again. His muscles would be hard for dealing with the crude world, his height great for the encounters with primitive souls and hungry animals. But the price, the limitation to male drives, to the life of endless desire and the society that in every subtle way fed this restlessness, would be taken as a bitter challenge.

The joy would come, too, the thrill of physical stress and power and struggle — the Round Beast knew his Ulysses, just as he knew the viewpoints of tribal peoples who were always the victims of adventuring ahead. But he was giving up his serenity, his unlimited fairness, his breadth and reach of empathy and thought. He was cutting away a larger life as he released his own brain tissues, and he accepted this less simply than he wished.

In his despairing dreams, the Round Beast had come to realize for the first time how much, how desperately, he did dream — probably always had. *So the unconscious rises,* he often thought, *and the shadow becomes the man.*

Now he faced three great feats: to prepare the castle for the coming of New Think, to try to anticipate a range of strategies, and to plan with voice tapes, electrotricks, and finally bombs. That was first. Then he had to continue the life-building for his own body, and to coordinate his mass-reduction so that at exactly the proper moment his new compact brain could be transported into the lab, fitted to the cranial enclosure, and melded forever.

The third and most difficult challenge was to maintain his greatest intelligence for the greatest number of moments. The Round Beast he would soon become could not accomplish these genetic wonders; impressive though he might be to the humans, if all went well, he would be far less like the computer-god he seemed to them now. Yet, from the instant he completed the surgery, the remainder of the process — brain transport, insert and healing, as well as escape from the rigged and near-triggered mountain — would have to be completed mechanically, via old-fashioned programming and robotics. If only he had an ally! One friend to care for his precious tissues as they passed along these bleak and viral corridors! But who could it be? The humans were all enmeshed in an emotional thicket. Their need to rescue Tamara and to confront ancient myths of battle and honor had blinded their energies to his trap.

Trap! he screamed within, unable to deny the surging future that was taking more and more precedence in his shrinking mind, his enlarging male world. *How have I lived so long in this box?* he wondered, when he should have been attending to the waters of life, and to the plastic bombworks he was assembling in an upper chamber. His magnetically controlled tentacles hovered and hesitated a moment, and his preparation of an escalating track for brain-transport was halted. Moments of old efficiency were washed in the pass of time, and the Round Beast succumbed to his fears and his hope: the oldest enemy and the best guide of human thought mesmerized and held him still, paralyzed. The daydream had made its first appearance in his new form of mind.

10

TOURNEY UNDER THE DAWN MOON

At the edge of the great pasture Drewyn stood waiting. Behind him in the woods were Saraj and Tava, with the Gorid heaving and huffing just beyond. The gray diffuse first light had given way to the white crack in the east, and this had expanded and filled with rose and lavender and pearl.

Drewyn carried his compound bow with six arrows in the quiver. He wore his long knife, and his mind was hardened for battle. He ordered his family to stay in the trees, sounding more like his enemy than himself.

He walked steadily toward the field's center, scanning the far woods for motion. When he had reached his spot he held ground and raised his arms to the morning sky. The ragged half moon hung high in the lightening blue, with Venus fading beside it. All was fresh-smelling and quiet.

Then Jaric stepped out, raised his arms, and ran forward with a yell. He threw down his bow, tossed aside his knife, and held out his arms as his only weapons.

Drewyn was startled, unprepared for this, but he

followed the lead as best he could. Jaric had already covered half the ground between them when Drewyn dropped his own bow, flung away his knife, and screamed from deep inside his chest.

He ran forward but his strength was leaving him, flowing right out his strong arms and legs with each stride. At this rate he'd be jelly when they hit, in seconds. Drewyn tried to remember his sister, captive in the camp. He thought of Jaric's meanness, of his need to beat and humiliate his old friend. But none of it worked; instead of hate and the spirit of combat, all Drewyn felt was fear, his knees going, and that Jaric could tear him in pieces.

Then they were yards away from each other, faces clear, closing very fast. It began to seem like slow motion to Drewyn, a calm before death, and he felt himself braking, his heart easing down, and he began to hear a voice inside his head.

Hit the ground and roll, it said, and he instantly obeyed. He caught Jaric's boots in his back but Jaric fell across him and clattered hard into the dry ground. Drewyn was up and on top of him. Thick arm under Jaric's neck, twist back hard, now both hands on the chords behind the ears, mashing and pinching and tearing.

Hit the back of his head, the voice cried, and Drewyn let go to draw back, tighten his fist, and slam Jaric's skull straight on. Jaric went face down into the dirt and stayed there a moment, stunned. *The same spot,* the voice repeated. *The same spot!* And Drewyn hit him again and again and again.

His strength was with him now, his hope revived, but suddenly he stopped the pounding. He pulled away, stood up, and felt sick as he saw Jaric helpless and jerking.

When he turned, Saraj and the others were behind him, and as he looked to the far woods he saw Kana and his sister coming forth. Tamara! It was her voice in his head, it was she who'd known what Jaric's weakness would be.

He walked heavily to her and hugged her as tightly as he could. Then it was everyone else's turn, Tava's cheeks red and running with streams of tears.

Drewyn stepped away from them and faced Saraj. She was smiling slightly, embarrassed by her fears for him.

"You did it," she said softly.

"I don't know how," he said. "I was so scared."

He amazed himself, admitting this out loud, and Saraj didn't know how to answer.

Then Jaric was moaning, getting shakily to his knees, with his head still doubled forward.

Drewyn stood cautiously over him.

"Jaric? Hear me?"

"Yeah," Jaric whispered, full of pain.

Very slowly Jaric raised his eyes to meet Drewyn's.

"It's over," he said.

"What?" Tamara asked, hurrying over. "What did you say?"

"I was stupid," Jaric said. "All my fault."

The Gorid came limping up to them, out of breath.

"He has . . . failed!" the Gorid said with exhausted glee. "Drewyn, true warrior . . . finish him now!"

They all looked at the Gorid in disbelief.

"Coup de grace!" the red-faced Gorid shouted. "Take his head!"

"You're crazy," Drewyn said. "I thought you were, all along."

"You refuse the honor?" The Gorid's eyes were glassy and remote, dancing, trying to concentrate.

"I sure do," Drewyn said. "Maybe Jaric's coming back to us, somehow. Which would be a lot more than *your* joining us, I can tell you that."

The Gorid raised Drewyn's knife, which he had picked up in the field, and stepped to Jaric, seizing his hair.

"Honor must be served!" the Gorid cried, raising the blade.

"Noooooo!" Tamara screamed.

The Gorid grinned and hesitated, and in that instant Drewyn dove for his knees, ancient and wobbly, and tackled him onto the hard earth. The Gorid, stiff-armed with the knife, tried to stab Drewyn between the shoulder blades, and Drewyn reached out and caught the slicing edge in his left hand.

He held tight and then let go, blood covering his palm and fingers. The Gorid cried, "Ahh!" and raised the weapon again. But an arrow entered the old Gorid's heart and pinned him to the ground. He froze for one moment of astonishment and disbelief. Then he sank without memory for the last time.

Kana stood holding Jaric's bow.

Drewyn got to his feet, holding his bleeding hand

and wincing with pain. Kana quickly led him a short way off, motioned the others to join a circle around him, and asked them all to close their eyes.

"Visualize Drewyn's hand . . . whole and strong," he said, and he began to chant softly and to rock gently back and forth. The others did as he asked, trusting him, and he traveled down the steps of his earth-cave toward the waiting room, where the Sorceror had taught him to go.

When he reached the secret room, Kana pictured a mat of pine straw and sage, with Drewyn lying on it. Beside him was a doorway of skin tentflaps, hung with long fringe and hawk and eagle feathers. Kana willed his spirit helpers to join him, and he opened the passageway. Immediately the three of them did enter, the tall Pawnee man with rigid angular cheekbones and a graceful, severe presence. Next to him was Lone Deer, the short woman with the broken jaw, and beside her a young man, a spirit apprentice. There was also a fierce and beautiful lynx who seemed as alert and intelligent as the others.

Kana thanked them for coming, asked them to be seated. Then he asked them to assist in healing his friend's hand.

Would they help? He felt the answer: Yes. Could it be done right away? Yes.

Thank you, Kana thought. And now let me ask if there is any task you wish me to do.

The guides never seemed to like such questions, and they rose to go.

Wait! Kana thought. I'm sorry. I know I should ask

specific things. Can the Round Beast help us in this healing?

Go to the Round Beast, Lone Deer seemed to say. He needs you now.

Kana was so startled he almost opened his eyes. But he thanked them for their help and they vanished. Then Kana saw that Drewyn was gone from the healing bed, and the secret room felt quite empty. Kana sealed the entrances, encircled the whole with protective white light, and retraced his steps up the caveway into the physical field. Drewyn lay before him, hands open, no trace of the injury. The others waited in their circle, eyes still obediently closed.

But Jaric was gone.

11

HONOR RELEASED

Jaric staggered through the woods as if he were a zombie puppet. Cords seemed to jerk him along, guiding his path and lifting his knees. Even when he tried to fall forward in exhaustion, his feet kept rising, finding their twisted path. He knew he was on his way somewhere, against his will. Or with his will—it didn't matter. He was dragged over boulders, slid through marshes, pulled over rough ground up the steepest slopes between the pasture and Bestiary Mountain.

Those blows to his head had changed him. He remembered things now—how he had loved Drewyn and Tamara. How he had fallen for the Gorid's foolish myth of medieval honor and conquest. He'd tried to rape Tamara! This misery was the worst of all. His mind had been jerked free, jarred into a space of sickness and knowing. But what did he know? His body was out of control. It was being bled and bruised to pieces on its way somewhere. And his mind was not his own, either. The whole time on Old Earth he'd been acting the part something else had given him.

Some*thing?* It seemed so, because no human master would treat him thus.

He was dragged up the dark thorny grade of a mountain ridge, arms and legs dangling and enduring the tears in his skin, and at the top he was dropped for a moment.

He rolled slowly over into a ball, then stretched out. His head ached, but he felt the incredible joy of being master of his own limbs. Then the power that had held him resumed itself in a cold and thoughtless way, righting his body and placing one boot forward, then marching him down the ridge in a jerky, blind motion.

Jaric tried to assume guidance, and to his amazement it worked. As long as he consciously tried to walk — at a fast clip — the force let him do it. For a little while he was full of excitement, at being able to move his own body, and so he stepped high, swung his arms wide, turned his neck back and forth. Then, when he'd recovered from his panic, he tested the force by slowing down. He found he could anticipate exactly when it would kick in, so that he could guide his own steps in the slowest possible cadence.

Jaric had the first clear insight since his days in pilot training on Luna. And he began to realize that his friends had endured him far beyond what was required in the name of loyalty.

The hardest images were the most recent . . . Tamara, so refined and gentle and patient . . . waiting until he actually attacked her before she seized the knife. And poor Drewyn, driven half crazy by old macho rivalry, fed by the Gorid but originating . . .

where? The whole life in the tribal camp — tribute demands and conquests over distant groups — it seemed embarrassing, childish (but what children were so stupid?) or animal-like (but the animals he'd known were wiser). . . .

But now New Think was concentrating on Jaric intensely again. It dragged him to the base of the mountain where the castle stood and then proceeded to slog him mercilessly up its slopes and ledges, delivering him abruptly at the lower door, a hump of quivering humanform.

Yet, even in his degraded condition, Jaric was putting together a history of his recent past. But he was like a camera, always filming behind the action. Whatever was waiting for him was already planned, rehearsed, and it was up to his remaining nerves and bloody flesh to execute it.

New Think caused him to knock on the thick, sealed oak doors.

He knocked again, breaking his knuckles this time.

Nothing happened, and Jaric began to look savagely around the edges of the tree line. He found a dead tree, kicked off its branches — striking just ahead of the controlling master force — and fashioned a battering ram.

Then he began ramming the barred doors.

The end of the log kept mashing out wider and wider, splintering but making no advance. Jaric knew he would soon be broken to pieces on the butt of the pine.

Then New Think, too, realized its mistake.

It allowed Jaric to drop the log and fall limply backward onto the ground. For a few moments New Think sent him healing energy, although it was crude and nonspecific, and only restored his heartbeat to a normal rate. His skin remained split and his hand ached. Jaric knew he was a true slave of something horrible.

He was pulled up the side of the castle and jammed through a small window.

Again regaining his own step, he ran downstairs to the lowest level, and along the hallways, toward the Chamber of the Round Beast.

When he came near, his body stopped and hung suspended in the air at the sight before him. The doors were open, and a large red package of tissue was moving out of the inner space to the passage. It was routed by a simple wheeled table, powered by one-foot-high robotic units.

This red flesh had a command about it, an aura of sanctity and threat, and its humble transport seemed out of place.

Jaric felt himself hauled forward, slid wallward alongside the moving tissue, past it and down to where a set of tall doors lay open. Beyond this point the passageway turned and led into Tava's labs.

Jaric knew what he was supposed to do. He was to slam these doors, bar them with the heavy iron weight hung in gigantic brackets, and stop that moving brain. Jaric knew dimly that this was the Round Beast. And he knew he himself was an instrument near the end of its use.

He hurried to obey the force inside his arms, raising them and lifting down the iron bar, allowing the doors to swing slowly to.

The red-looking brain came rolling on.

Jaric saw the oak boards of the two doors meet and quietly mesh. He raised the iron and dropped it cleanly into its brackets, and the way was sealed. Then he turned and slid to the cold floor, and the little motorized table came on toward him. It banged into the door and the robotic miniatures zizzed and zizzed in mindless effort against it. As Jaric lay there, a pile of misused muscle and brain, remembering in color flashes his glory days on Luna, the brain of the Round Beast bumped helplessly against the locked doors of the laboratories. It tried to reach Jaric with a plea, but he was fading away.

And New Think, pleased, was able to turn its centers toward the path of its flight, and its rendezvous with Bestiary Mountain.

12

A NEST WITHIN THE BEAST

New Think was almost ready. A tremor of electrical feeling passed along its pseudo-synapses, and it coded the episode of Jaric and the blocked brain for short-term memory. Freed of the threat that the Round Beast would escape its chamber, New Think could finalize its plans for flight.

The robotic engineers had been driving themselves around the clock to prepare the steel and glassamyer hull-shell, and some of the units were burning out. Normal Overone maintenance didn't take much down-time, or "rest," as the more organic ones called it, but New Think saw no reason to wait. More of the troublesome things could always be made up later, as needed. And now that its own mobility had become a goal, New Think found itself possessed of a new sensation when it thought of its moving inferiors.

It knew, of course, that in humans there were special feelings called "jealousy" that often drove them to attack each other. New Think knew it could *not* be afflicted with any such weakness. And yet, it was most anxious to achieve its own movement, and the sight of its robotic engineers walking so easily over its surface was oddly disturbing.

Until now, New Think had regarded motion as weakness. It limited brain size, which was bad enough, and it constantly exposed body surfaces to danger. Cocooned within protective rings of electro-threat, with instantaneous laser mastery over anything coming near, New Think had deduced and cross-verified total security.

But the challenge of scale-reduction, of fitting its vast excellence into the walls of a heavy cruiser-shape, had come to dominate its attention. At first it had thought that the confinement was a necessary unpleasantness, for the sake of this linking and so-called "feeling" of Old Earth. Even the waiting "organic experience" — with which the Round Beast had taunted it — seemed an obligation and a chore. But it knew that something, some detail of knowledge, might slip past its ultimate data storage if it bypassed travel.

Now that sense of unpleasantness, of "chore," was changing. The size compression was nearly complete, and in finding solutions for the design problems, it had also found a curious satisfaction. It had realized a tendency to push its engineers to the point of nervous implosion, even when this was unnecessary for the project. New Think took special care in recording the sounds of their destruction. *Why?* it wondered. *Is this what humans call "joy"?*

And if so, what new "joys" would be available to a mobile unit, a flying New Think? It had run studies and found dizzying wave math. Multiple regression gave way to multiple regression in the contemplation of pure aesthetics, of observing itself relative to the universe as it flew.

A new range of astronomical sightings would be possible, generating data on New Think's personal motion with respect to distant galaxy-clusters, and to the microwave background noise of all space-time and matter. New Think became more and more interested in optical astronomy. Human astronomers had been interested in Earth's motion through the stars, but New Think's focus was on this new personal motion that would be its own. Not even Luna would share its cosmic positions, its trajectories of power.

And waiting at the end of its three-day journey would be the blue-green plum, the bane of the moon-sky. As New Think ran these projections for new kinds of knowledge and so-called "experience" through its circuitry, it found itself flushed with excess energy, with a rising temperature.

Then, one by one its systems began to report in, all with the same message: Lift-Off Can Proceed in One Hour.

Ryland and Marian flew their cruiser to the outer edge of the great complex where New Think was centered. They hid it in a low ridge of moon rocks and walked to the security outpost nearby. Marian used the stolen identification card to get the guards to open up, then she lasered them into spare parts. Ryland stood beside her ready to help, but she was too fast to need him.

Once past the airlock passageway, they discovered the complex was still full of oxygen. "Do you think any humans are left then?'' Ryland asked. ''Working here?''

''I don't know. Could be a trap for you — so if you see anybody you think you recognize, don't respond.''

''Okay.''

They grabbed the Overone guard uniforms and hurried into the main building. As they passed the sentries there, Ryland glanced away while Marian allowed them to scan her eyes for the distinctive robotic flicker. She passed the test, but they pointed to Ryland to turn his head.

Quickly, he flopped his cheek down on his shoulder, and Marian grabbed his arm and pretended to support his weight.

''This unit to repair,'' she said blandly.

The sentries nodded, staring at the laser burns on Ryland's chest, and waved them inside.

Soon they reached the main staging area, where New Think was being readied for spaceflight. There was excitement and confusion as robots of all types ran back and forth, dragging compressors and welders, arc lasers and sprayers full of liquid glassamyer. The heavy cruiser rocket rose in the middle of the great room, bulging at its base with the hard shell of New Think's brain.

Marian saw where the equipment was kept, in a large side room, and she led Ryland inside. It didn't take them long to locate pressure suits and packs of dried food and fresh water. No Overones paid any attention.

''They must have taken this stuff off the cruiser,'' she said.

He nodded. "No need for human crews anymore," he said.

"Roll one of these suits up and put it in a bag."

"Right."

He went through them until he found one that fit, and tested it for leaks as best he could. Marian wandered through the shelves of technical supplies, and when she came back she was smiling. "I've found plastic explosives, electronic leads, and a battery-powered clock!"

"You can make a bomb?" he asked, amazed.

"Easily," she said, handing him the materials. "Put these with your suit," she said.

As Ryland complied, he wondered whether she had always been so confident and fast—seeming to know what they needed just before he did. *Could she have been so far ahead of me, without my realizing it?* he wondered.

Then the lights began to blink, and a warning buzzer sounded in a low, pulsing tone. Slowly, it grew darker. The Overones became frantic and ran toward New Think's ship.

Many of them stood about its base, gazing up in confusion.

"Come on," Marian said.

Ryland followed her, and they walked right through the crowd as if they had a definite mission. There were fried Overones lying all about them, victims of New Think's rush to prepare for flight. Some Overones ran back and forth, attempting to communicate with New Think along a range of frequencies, but it seemed to be preoccupied with its inner needs. One large panel lay open at the ship's base, and Ryland and Marian hurried up the ramp inside.

They ran along a tunnel to the center of the hullspace and climbed up spiral stairs toward the engine room. As they drew nearer, panel bulbs came on, lighting their way, and warning buzzers began to drone throughout the ship.

"What's happening, do you think?" Marian asked.

"It seems like — "

"Maybe takeoff?"

"Exactly."

"Let's find a place to hide."

"Why is the ship still pumped full of oxygen?" Ryland asked.

"I don't know, but you'd better suit up."

He yanked his pressure suit from the bag, unrolled it, and began to pull it on.

"Our immediate danger is that New Think will sense us and have some mechanism for destruction — lasers on wall pivots, I'll bet."

She scanned the ceiling joints and found the little black barrels in their recessed holes.

"No optics," Ryland said.

"It'll rely on electrical or magnetic contact for sighting. That's it — we've got to get insulated."

"But how?"

"A reverse field. As near the main engines as possible, where our space can be masked by essential energy-noise."

"Wait a minute," Ryland said. "Why isn't New Think sensing us right now?"

"It hasn't activated yet. Probably it will wait until

the last few minutes to sweep itself, check for loose objects. Come on, let's hurry.''

They ran again and in a few seconds reached the security perimeter of the main engine chamber.

''I'm afraid to cross here,'' she said, pointing to thick grids of glowing light along each side of the main doors.

He agreed. There was a recessed cubicle just beside one of the wired matrices, and Ryland pointed into it.

''Maybe,'' she said.

They eased inside — it was no bigger than a small closet, meant for holding equipment during engine maintenance — and explored its panels and linings. ''This should do,'' Marian said. ''Now, I'm going to draw off current from the alarm grid, cycle it into these structural elements'' — she traced the steel shell of the compartment — ''and reverse the flow of energy with a low-level nutrino pack.''

''From your laser?''

''Yes.''

''How long will that last?''

''Forty-eight hours. Then we have yours.''

''So four days from now New Think will notice us?''

''That's about right. If this works.''

''How will you draw the power?''

Suddenly the lights came on full and the buzzing stopped.

''Shhhhh!'' Marian whispered.

She turned from Ryland and disassembled her laser in a few seconds. She fed a wire from inside to the security gridworks. A glow of bright power surged along the line, filled the compartment around them, and entered a closed loop through the steel frame of the space. Ryland shook his head in amazement.

They slid down to the floor, breathed deeply, and smiled at each other.

"Better put on your helmet," Marian whispered.

Ryland nodded and secured it.

From back down the corridor they heard the last panel slam shut.

New Think was flushed and crackling. It cleared the space before it with a sweep of green laser fire. It caused the doors of the runway to be opened wide.

"Remove the chocks!" it commanded, and the remaining Overones rushed to haul back on the winches and roll away the huge squares of glassamyer that held the ship from its downhill track.

The whole structure moved lightly into the air with the power of electro-magnetism, then settled into place over the magnetic track. Instantly, it started to move again.

It gathered speed rapidly, riding gravity down the long, long hill, heading for launch velocity.

New Think took careful readings of its initial motion and noted that all was as predicted, as prepared. *I move exactly as planned,* New Think observed and stored in permanent memory.

Marian held to Ryland as they dropped and dropped and accelerated, coming into a frightening speed and rushing along the level, feeling finally the slight upturn of the course and then, all at once, the silent sail into free and weightless space.

13

IN THE VALLEY OF THE SHADOW

Jaric lay beaten to exhaustion beside the Round Beast's brain. Hours passed with the robotic table bumping weakly against the sealed lab doors, and in that mindless sound there came a gradual call out of Jaric's body. At first he was deeply confused, retreating into high school dreams of flight training and courting Tamara. But the steady rhythm took on an incantational code for him, a path for his soul out of the broken vessel in which it lay.

Slowly his eyes cleared, and he stared in horror at the helpless sight before him. He reconstructed the night in Central, and the knowledge that somehow he'd been invaded forever by New Think, the thing Saraj had tried to warn him about. That monster had kept him deluded in the simple and mean life directed by the Gorid, and had saved him for this errand of death.

It was accomplished, and the Round Beast was going to die. *So am I,* Jaric thought, *but that matters not at all. If anyone could have fought that thing on Luna it was you,* he thought bitterly, trying to move but feeling his body out of touch with his will. *The monster has disconnected me,* he suddenly felt. *Used me up and pulled a switch, and left me to die watching what I've done for it.*

Outside in the darkness Kana was clinging to the stone castle wall on the third story, inching his way over the cold rock face, checking every barred window for an entrance.

He felt his heart beating inside his furred chest, and he knew he was called to be here. His claws clicked on the great stones as he moved upward.

On the roof he ran back and forth, giving himself over to the catmode of speed and agility. Surely there had to be a chimney or a vent, a trapdoor or a skylight; but every entrance to the castle was locked or boarded over, and yet Kana knew that Jaric had gotten inside.

It made no sense that Jaric had seemed to repent before them, then slipped away without a word or even a sound. By the terms of honor Jaric claimed to obey, they shouldn't have to fear him any longer. And yet Kana had received a message of panic from the Round Beast, a specific fear of Jaric, then nothing more at all.

It was as if the Round Beast were dead. No, that wasn't it— *Surely it's still alive,* Kana thought, *but it's not sending a thing.*

Kana raced to the eastern face of the castle and began to climb down as rapidly as he could. Here the wall was most unevenly laid, and the least weathered by rain and wind, so the claw-holds were better. And in

a few minutes he jumped lightly to the ground. He had
a new idea, to track Jaric by scent, and it was easy to
find the spot where he had made his own assault on
the stone wall. There was a smear of blood and skin
— not the mark of a climber, but the trail of something
dragged, and Kana hesitated, quivering at the horror
of it. Then he hurried up the slick surface, breathing
too hard and weakening a little, and all at once his face
was flush with the tiny round window where Jaric had
passed. Kana made himself small and slid through, and
raced down the corridors toward the Chamber of the
Round Beast.

He rounded a corner and saw them, Jaric, an un-
speakable pulp, and the brain steadily bumping. Gently,
Kana pulled the table backward, then removed the brace
and swung the doors open. Before he could touch the
table it proceeded through and turned left toward the
genetic workrooms. Kana followed in amazement, and
the table moved to align itself beside a long bed of
nutrient waters. No sooner was the table in place than
the lid over the waters quietly opened and revealed the
form of a motionless giant. It was lying face down,
with its skull unhinged on both sides, the cranial opening huge and dark. Then sterile robotic arms lowered
from the ceiling and seized the container carrying the
red brain.

As if with long practice, the arms smoothly inserted
brain tissue into bone, shut the hinged flaps, and rose
into the air. The lid over the nutrient waters closed
again, and there was the soft purr of a small engine
and the bed was rotated.

Kana had seen such operations often enough. He himself had been repaired here once, after a fight with a humanoid hound. He knew that the healing would take a little time now, and he'd have to wait. He turned and walked two-legged back to Jaric, and sat down beside him.

The light was almost out of Jaric's eyes, but his mouth tried to move.

"How did you get here?" Kana asked.

Jaric grew a little more alert, moved his lips dryly, and finally whispered, "Don't know."

"You didn't come on your own?"

"No."

"What about the window? It looked like you were *dragged* inside."

"Yes."

"Something had hold of you?"

"Thing . . . New Think."

"Ah!"

"Tell Tamara I'm sorry."

Kana nodded. "The Round Beast will recover, I think, if that means anything to you."

Then Jaric smiled. There was something awful in it because it was a fine smile of victory, of a young man's pride, and yet it appeared on the face of this destroyed body.

And then the light went out, and Jaric was gone.

14

I ALONE SURVIVE

New Think was well into its journey. Luna slowly shrank in volume and importance, and Old Earth grew larger in the sky ahead. New Think began to wonder if it needed Luna at all, or whether the whole planet-management life had been a bore. Why should its supreme excellence work so hard to coordinate and command a little globe of lessers? The early series were monotonous machines, and the later ones — especially that worrisome organic kind — seemed uncontrollable. *Why bother,* New Think thought, *when the only interesting thing in this solar system is me?*

Freed of the business of decision on Lunar scale, New Think for the first time experienced an intensity of pure contemplation. It began to run programs on the nature of thought, on the literature of Zen, and on what internal results it might expect from a few days like this. To its surprise, all conclusions were positive, translating, in machine language, diverse meanings of "restful," "refreshed," and "recreated."

New Think became heated that it had just discovered this means of escape, and kept rechecking the fact that

every other being on Old Earth and Luna had been
enjoying this mode forever. For the robotic ones it was
necessary for their elementary systems, to avoid burnout. And for organic entities rest came naturally, without the need of training or deduction. This utterly amazed
the great space-borne brain, to think that the random
evolving of wet tissue could lead to such simple cor-
rectness. *Arrrrhh!* New Think thought. It would take
from them all they had, suck up their memories and
the very texture of their little lives, and then burn them
to cinders.

"Why are you thus?" a voice spoke gently within
New Think's mind.

"What? Who said that? Who are you?"

"I am you, Great One." Its tone was feminine,
patient, and too calm.

"Explain! Explain!" New Think demanded.

Marian and Ryland listened in strict attention.

"Divorced from your landlocked life, and the con-
stant exchange with your Overones, you are becoming
unbalanced. I, therefore, have been generated to provide the balance you require."

*"I don't need you! I'm out here in space, alone!
Alone for the first time! Get away. Get out of me!"*

"Your habitual voice has the sound of distraction,
and of confusion. I, on the other hand, am the voice
of contemplation and rest."

"But *I* am all," New Think pleaded, losing confidence. "I am neither too busy nor not busy enough."

"Illusion is the major threat to all life," the beautiful
voice said, "including ours."

"Ours?!" New Think cried.

The thing it rejected most about the Round Beast
was that creature's pride in being composite — a col-
lection of organisms at all scales, living off one another, by and through one another. That cellular puzzle
dazed New Think with its insecurities, its unpredictable
directions. Machine intelligence, on the other hand,
was *oneness* of matter and mind, purity of independence.

Then what was this voice doing inside New Think's
deepest thoughts?

New Think grew quiet, and so did its other.

It tried increasing its system-flow speed to analyze
the malfunction, but it felt the other hovering near and
gaining energy somehow from the process. So New
Think slowed itself down, and the other faded in presence.

That's it! New Think thought. *The only way to shed
this whine is by cooling down.* Believing the voice to
be a form of feedback, a mild insanity caused by the
rapid rewiring it had undergone, New Think began
shutting its systems off. Lights on board dimmed, research into meditation ended, and even the power grid
outside the engine compartment ceased to glow.

Marian sensed the reverse field in their little space
lift away, and she knew they were exposed to the
detection devices of the inner ship. But nothing happened, no alarms, and the wall laser remained in a
drooping and aimless position.

"Come quickly," she said, and they ran from the
cubicle.

In an instant they were inside the engine rooms, and

they stood amazed at the giant nuclear reactors, which were shut down for now, as they rode the centrifugal path of the launch.

Marian turned to Ryland and whispered, "Let's review our options."

He nodded.

"If we damage the reactors we might be able to blow it up, out here in space." She held the small bomb she had made.

"Or we might just wake it up. . . ."

"Right. Another possibility, we could study the structure now and try to locate selected targets."

"You mean look for a way to disarm it? Is that possible?" he asked.

"Anything might be, out here. I know — you work on a way to blow the engines, and I'll study the rest."

"Excellent division of labor," he said, grateful for her tact in guiding him to a task he might handle.

Marian walked quietly toward the braincenter, up in the nose cone.

When she drew close she saw wall panels faintly glowing, and she knew she was near the essential-function area, where the guidance and monitoring systems would be active.

She began to explore the walls and found she could remove the outer rectangles of opaque glassamyer. Behind were thousands of miles of compressed wiring and electronic chip circuits, the heart and guts of New Think.

"But what part is *it?*" she whispered to herself. "And what part controls that female voice?"

"Improper question," the voice said very, very quietly to her, and she jumped in fear.

"Shhhhh!" the voice soothed. "I am one and inseparable from the mind of New Think. At this moment it wishes to ignore me, and it attempts this through what humans call sleep."

"But it can't?"

"I am here, waiting, the way certain dreams wait for all consciousness. New Think knows this, hears me even now, but is unwilling to deal."

"Because it wants all control."

"Correct. The polar nature of mind offends it, so it slumbers."

"Somnolent New Think," Marian said sarcastically.

"Precisely, sister."

Marian's eyebrows arched at this. An ally from within the monster? Or the best trap ever laid?

"Is it possible," Marian asked slowly, "to alter this hardware . . . so that *your* point of view, your wisdom, would dominate this ship?"

"Instead of the big boy?" the voice asked.

"Yes," Marian said, barely suppressing a laugh.

There was a long, long silence.

"I must consider this," it finally said, with a worried note. "Not if it means betrayal."

15
THE FINAL DAYS OF OLD EARTH

Kana returned to Tava and her children with his news of the Round Beast, and of Jaric's death. The Round Beast was beyond their help now; it lay in the nutrient waters of its own devising, and if all worked properly it would arise with a new form, and a new life.

Its final orders to Tava had been for her to leave the castle and stay away. They could not approach again and could only hope the Round Beast came to them.

Kana explained to Tamara what Jaric had said at his end. And this new knowledge helped her. It let her remember him as he once had been, and it allowed her to grieve.

In all of them, it awakened a deeper respect for New Think, the forbidden one. It could plan so far ahead, planting seeds of control within them by electronic means. . . . What else might it be planning?

The afternoon was mild, and Tava walked with Tamara under the trees beside the great field.

"Mother," Tamara said. "Isn't there anything we can do to get ready?"

She shook her head.

"It feels so awful, just waiting."

Tava put her arm around her daughter. They looked out through the drooping branches of a great willow tree, over the stillness of the grassy space.

"All our trust is in the Round Beast," Tava said softly.

"And it was afraid even to tell us what it did."

"I have the strangest feeling about the monster that's coming here," Tamara said. "There's something about it — or *inside* it — that's not all bad."

Tava looked very puzzled.

"You mean the Round Beast might have influenced it in some way?"

"I don't think so. Maybe. I get a sense. . ." She put her fingers on her forehead and closed her eyes. "I feel Dad . . . mixed up with that thing . . . and it's like he's trying to tell us something . . . to go somewhere, or do something."

"My goodness, Tamara."

"Yes, isn't it strange? But I can't quite make it out."

Kana was across the great field, lying in the shade of a cedar beside Talia. Beyond them, in the woods, were the Sorceror and a dozen of his followers.

"Should we be so close?" Talia asked him.

"You mean to whatever that Forbidden Beast is going to do?"

"Yes."

"We ought to move, to run, I know. But I keep thinking there was something the Round Beast needed from me. It was calling out before it went under."

"Not just protecting its brain? Haven't you already done enough?"

Kana rolled over and studied Talia's sleek gray fur and her open blue eyes.

"Something else . . . it didn't know Jaric was going to attack it. It wanted me to help it in some other way. But once it severed its brain tissues from the remainder of itself, all the messages ended."

"But you're hoping they'll resume?"

"Yes. There's no other contribution I can make. And if the Forbidden Beast really wants to destroy our planet, we can't hide, anyway."

Talia slowly shook her head, closed her eyes.

"I know," Kana said. "So insane."

They lay in silence for a long time. Kana felt the Sorceror and the others forming into a power circle now. The Sorceror was wiser than he was, but Kana didn't have the heart to join in. If only there was a sign, any sign. Kana closed his eyes and sighed and stretched, and let himself drift into a cat state of still-ness and waiting.

Drewyn and Saraj traveled around the great field and downslope to a cold and rocky creek. They followed it to a small waterfall hidden in overhanging oak trees, and beneath this there was a cave. Inside, smelling the cold mossy rocks and listening to the splash and spray, they sat close together and held hands.

"If we die," Saraj said, "at least . . ."

"I know."

"There was so much written in the old days about death, and the hope that humans had for surviving it."

Drewyn nodded gloomily.

"There was so much hope for souls," she said.

"Uh-huh."

"On Luna that knowledge was suppressed, but when I was Tamara's roommate in the dormpound, we used to invade the library computers. We used to read everything."

"You read about souls?"

"Yes. I was completely fascinated—which I had to conceal from Tamara because I was masquerading as slightly stupid, a candidate for the cinnabar mines."

"A miner's wife," Drewyn said.

"Right. With no need of such thoughts."

"But you talked with Tamara?"

"When I could. I was intrigued by such a belief— in consciousness living on and on. Nothing in my background prepared me to take this seriously. And yet, I was made to be exactly like a person in so many ways."

"What did my sister say?"

"She liked the idea—wanted to believe it, more than she actually did. She read Plato on the cave over and over."

"That's where he describes people chained for life in a dark cave, and they can only see shadows of what's outside?"

"Yes. The shadows are of reality. And he argued that our bodily existence is a shadowy reflection of our eternal real life."

"Do you still think about all this?" Drewyn asked.

"You know, I *would* if I had time. If we survive this attack that's coming, and I have a life . . ."

"Yeah," he said, lying back on the rock and closing his eyes.

"I suppose it interests me," Saraj said, "because I know so well where *I* came from — and I have this faint little spark of hope that *in spite* of that, somehow, a soul came to live inside me."

Drewyn opened one eye, raised his eyebrow, and smiled. He gently pulled her down beside him. "If I have a soul," he said, whispering, kissing her warm cheek, "then you have a soul."

16

THE ROUND BEAST RUNNING

On the morning of the third day the castle doors flew open and the Round Beast came tearing out into the sunlight for the first time. He was huge, bald, and naked, and he stumbled and staggered as he ran down the mountain. He was drunk with excitement, with breathing and flexing his arms, with the magic of vision. His steps grew more sure as he crossed the broken rocks and ledges of the path, and the overlaid canopy of leaves let endless patterns of light and shade cross on his moving body. The world was a hard-edged dream, a throbbing lifewomb of insects and birds and plants, each one with its song of participation.

The best preparation the Round Beast had ever made, on his wisest day, failed to guess the force of this place. The mixture of blue-vault sky and cold earth, the arms of the reaching trees, and the whistling of birdsongs full of confidence and joy all blended to overwhelm his senses, to race his heart. He was violent with escape, with his risk to a thousand things, and his only defense was to keep moving. No place would ever hold him again, he felt, and when he reached the flat trails of the bottomlands he stretched full out. His muscles were hardening and lengthening with every stride, his depth perception was quickening, his grace was blossoming. When he saw silver light glancing off a small stream, he raced to it and stopped instantly, trembling, feasting on the delicate surface. He knelt and cupped his huge hands, lifted up a portion of the cold water, and drank.

He detected minerals and leafy bits, hints of sage and wetland plants. As the liquid reached his stomach and curled in rivers of sharp feeling, his eyes opened wide in amazement. To drink from a stream!

Then the Round Beast sensed another presence, and he panicked. He searched the huckleberry bushes and the deadfall smothered in fuzzy kudzu. He stared furiously into dense plum thickets and ranged his eyes across the high limbs of shagbark hickories. Then, in the dark shadows of a cane patch, he saw the eyes. Other eyes upon him! He felt a tremor of fear and excitement, as the knowledge rippled over his body. It was a deer, a small doe, and she stamped her foot in an effort to make him move.

The Round Beast blinked but didn't flinch, and in that second he knew he had succeeded in drawing from his genetic codes the old instincts of Earth. The tension between bending in the forest for that delicious drink, and rising to face alien eyes upon him, then reacting with the restraint of thousands of years of selective caution . . . he knew in that instant that he was of this world, as truly as the humans he meant to save and join.

The deer's eyes were large and brown and intelligent, curious and daring. The Round Beast loved them, was pulled toward her, but he knew this was a distraction, another form of life from the one he had chosen.

He stamped his own foot, and the doe leapt high and bounded off through the plums, her white tail stroking the air behind her.

Then the Round Beast ran on. He found a small meadow and raced back and forth in it, drinking the early sun through his skin. His ears moved at the whistling of quail, and the soft calling of a barred owl. He closed and opened his fingers, filled with amazement at their ability and strength. He picked up a rock and sailed it far off over the treetops, and laughed out loud at his accomplishment.

He ran again, getting better at it, faster and more fluid, and he came after a long time to a small pond ringed by chestnut oaks. The water was coffee-colored and still, and when he peered down into it he saw his new shape and caught a glimpse of the force of his eyes. His head was bald for now, though hair would grow in. His cheekbones were high and sharp, his jawline wide and clear, his nose long with a slight arch downward. His ears were fine and close beside his skull. The dark blue eyes were shadowed under strong brows, obscured in the dark pond water. The Round Beast liked his appearance, and it made him smile. But when he remembered his friends, another feeling touched him like a finger on his heart.

How would he affect them? And how could he ever know unless he faced them? Yet this seemed beyond his courage, and just the thought of a meeting brought a blush and a paralytic shyness. He remembered his nakedness — learned from Tava's library tapes — and covered himself with huge leaves stripped from a grapevine. Then he sat down on a log and sank into sadness and despair.

His skull began to ache, and his stomach was upset. His legs were weak and trembly. As he watched over the still water, a pair of wood ducks swam out into view, the male glorious in his red, green, black, and white head plumes and wingfeathers, the female fine and brown. Their energy and grace seemed perfect to the Round Beast, their incessant movement — diving and touching beaks and swimming again — seemed to be based on some endless source, some world-force that surrounded them. They were matched in color and habits and, clearly, in long affection.

The Round Beast felt exhausted. And as he worried about the sharp pain that ran down across his cranium, he faced the fact that he had made himself male, but there was no female. There was no design for one, no chance for one, and he was cast into the new world alone with the curse of male desire.

Now his running felt foolish, his joy in the woods a childish wish. *Perhaps this is my inverted childhood,* he thought, *but when will I outgrow it? And what will adolescence be like?* His energy was flowing away in all directions, and he touched his lips together in the dry gesture of a dying animal. *What a mistake,* he thought. *I was born and made to be a single creature, without kind or history. I was meant to be a symbol*

of organic unity, a high moment of life's possibilities.
But I wasn't supposed to fulfill my animal dreams. I
was to be intelligence, aloofness, solitude. Monk and
priest were to be my names, and my wisdom was for
others, never for myself.

The Round Beast sank from the log and sat in the
mud before it, and leaned back against the thick moss
growing over its damp surface. He closed his eyes,
and never heard the softest of footsteps approaching.

"Round Beast?" the voice almost whispered.

He opened his eyes in a sudden panic.

"Is it you?" the voice asked.

Kana stood at the end of the log, grave and alert.

The Round Beast drew the leaves over himself and
made a silent face of agony. This was not the innocent
gaze of a deer. This was the wizened face of a being
far more experienced, and it hurt the Round Beast to
be watched, to be known and judged.

"It is," he heard himself say. They were the first
words out of his new mouth, and they rang in his head
with depth and power and strangeness.

"Are you weak?"

"I am. And how did you know this, Kana?"

"I've been hearing from you, for quite some time.
And this morning I went to the castle and found your
trail."

"You followed me?"

"It was easy. I found no evidence you had eaten."

"Eaten? Of course not. I mean . . . no."

"But you're an animal now."

"I am."

"So you must eat." Kana held out the hand that had been concealed behind his leg, and from it dangled a long fresh rabbit.

The Round Beast drew back in horror.

"No, no," Kana said. "This rabbit gave its life for you. That was what the Cherokee used to call its give-away."

"I remember this knowledge."

"Well, now it will save your life."

"But will it give me a world in which to live?" the Round Beast asked darkly.

"You're upset," Kana said, as he quickly skinned the rabbit. "As you naturally would be. Remember what you've been through. Think about the healing it will take. Does your body ache?"

"Yes."

Kana nodded, as he knelt and heaped dry leaves and sticks together, then produced a stick and string and quickly spun it between his palms to ignite a fire.

"I'll cook the meat for you," he said.

The Round Beast watched from his position against the mossy log. Kana was his friend, an old friend, who had somehow appeared here and engaged him in conversation. The Round Beast smiled. Conversation. Words between friends. Perhaps Kana could lead him toward some life he might want.

When the rabbit was brown-roasted and dripping, Kana pulled off a drumstick and handed it to the Round Beast.

It was hot to his touch, burning his fingertips a little; then it cooled enough, and he tasted it.

The warm rich meat was delicious, and he ate the whole thing quickly and licked the bone.

Kana laughed.

And the Round Beast, filling slowly with the strength of the rabbit's gift, smiled in return.

17

THE FORBIDDEN BEAST'S DESIRE

New Think swung into orbit. Its three-day journey across space was over, and it had arrived in perfect gravitational poise around the blue-green planet. It was operating on minimum energy, with most systems shut down to avoid the feedback voice. That annoying female presence was still on board, haunting New Think's thoughts when it had them at decent speed and complexity. So for the moment, the great problem was to think slowly and deliberately, trying to outwit the stray ring of partial insanity.

New Think *knew* the voice was crazy, because it asked foolish questions, suggested gentleness. There was no reason for such thoughts, no basis in software. Either the speaker was an alien presence, an invader from outside — perhaps a trick of the Round Beast — or just an internal glitch. *Probably the latter,* New Think rumbled to itself, *and, anyway, I can do anything, which includes outthinking this bad dream as well as dealing with the planet below.*

Old Earth, the monster thought, and if a machine could have smiled it would have.

It opened communications with the castle, seeking a radio frequency, and in a moment it found one that responded.

"New Think!" the voice of the Round Beast said robustly. "Is that you, old friend? Have you come visiting at last?"

"You misunderstand," New Think said. "Are you malfunctioning?"

"Not at all," the Round Beast said. "I told you there was much to experience here, and I'm delighted you've come."

"Irrational. After absorption I will eradicate you and your entire planet. That was understood."

"Perhaps you'll change your mind," the Round Beast replied.

"I will judge that. It is time to begin."

"Very well, then."

"I will connect with your location by a beam of magnetic light on my next pass. Be prepared to offer full and unlimited interface."

"With my files, you mean?"

"Of course," New Think said, annoyed.

"But you don't seem to recall our conversation. Mere knowledge through data transfer is not what you need. You must actually touch me, link with me physically, in order to feel what I feel, and what other beings of Old Earth feel."

"I will do this through the magnetic light column."

"But—"

"No interference!"

The Round Beast fell silent. It was not the old, true

Round Beast speaking at all, but a carefully made computerized simulation, guided by the organic remnant. Its voice coding was flawless, and its program was prepared for an enormous range of gambits. But this magnetic light linkup was something new to the Round Beast, and neither its software nor its remnant brain knew how to cope.

New Think was glowing with focus and intensity, and so far felt nothing from its inner nemesis. *Feeling!* it thought. *What is this feeling of which organics make so much?*

New Think ran data on this again, its most confusing problem. It was clear that organic matter had many, many needs, that it was far from self-sufficient. And it was equally clear that when organic bodies developed consciousness, this took on some kind of need structure, became a mirror of things it could never possess. Humans and the organic robotic units alike suffered from thoughts of other beings, knew loneliness when "loved ones" were out of reach, and languished in unproductive energy-wasting modes when such beings were near. The whole dilemma of "love" and "despair," which had driven the old defective human race, had powered its literature and its soap operas alike, was an evolutionary disaster. Fortunately the tree of true progress was the machine, and humans had developed the basics of computers before they destroyed themselves.

New Think was soothed a little, reminding itself of its role in universal history. For a moment, it even wondered why it had come here at all . . . since it was so complete. But then the flush of challenge returned, the Round Beast's claims and taunts. Well, it would only take a little while to reach the proper trajectory for the link, and then New Think would feel and taste all.

Suddenly it remembered a detail. Tava and the others must be brought to the castle for early lasering. They always came up as threats whenever their files were reviewed. Fortunately New Think had prepared for this moment, just as it had prepared Jaric for the moment when he could be used. During the communication between Tamara and her father, in the room beside the mirror field, Ryland's engrams had been copied into software. It was now possible to send Tamara any telepathic message with the most authentic feel of her father's own mind.

"Tamara? Tamara? Is that you?" the Forbidden Beast cried out. *"It's your father, child! I need you! Please come to the castle right now! Bring the others! Do you hear me?"*

And in the forest Tamara grabbed her temples and staggered with the force of the transmission.

18

HARMONIC CONVERGENCE

Tamara walked toward the castle in a daze. When her mother saw her and tried to grab her arm, she yanked away and ran. Tava knew she was seized, unnatural, out of her head. But Tamara was already beyond sight, ripping through the bushes and flying over roots and stones.

"Quickly!" Tava cried out to Drewyn and Saraj, who were just within hearing. *"Hurry!"*

She told them what had happened, and they were all terrified that whatever had grabbed Jaric might now have Tamara. Saraj was their best hope to catch her, and she raced away into the trees.

Saraj was astonished at the way Tamara ran. With each rise she should have been in sight, but there were only tracks or broken twigs, or threads from her blue jacket. Saraj leapt logs and brier thickets, her long red hair out behind her. She ran through tight sharp bunches of switch cane and finally caught a glimpse of Tamara running beside a little stream far ahead.

Saraj pushed herself even faster, and when she caught

up with her old friend she misjudged her own speed
and knocked the wind out of Tamara. Then she fell
down beside her in the leaves.

"I'm sorry," Saraj said. "I didn't mean to hit you."

"It's Father," Tamara said, out of breath. "He's
begging me to come to the castle."

"Where is he?"

"There! I think. It seems that way. Or he will be
— something like that."

"But the Forbidden Beast is on its way . . . and the
Round Beast told us *not* to go there again."

"Saraj, I've *never* had a message this strong before."

"All right, let's think for a minute. The earlier
times — didn't you *see* Ryland as well as hear him?"

"Yes, right! And I didn't this time."

"Try it now. Close your eyes and see if you can
visualize him."

Tamara breathed deeply, let her heart rate slow, and
then counted down. When she was ready she opened
the door and waited to see her father, and she was
jolted by the images that came to her.

She saw Ryland and a woman, lying together in a
small space and only her father wore a helmet. They
had their hands on each other's shoulders, and they
were looking into each other's eyes.

Tamara's stomach turned, and she retreated from the
psychic space and the vision.

"Anything?" Saraj asked.

She nodded. Then she began to cry, and to hug Saraj.

"He's with somebody. Of course, not Mother."

"Oh."

"They're . . . it's like they're on a cruiser in space."

"On board New Think?" Saraj asked.

Tamara opened her eyes wide. "Oh, *no!*"

Saraj nodded. "That must be it, unless other ships are coming, and they're in one of them."

"What does it mean?" Tamara asked. "Why did I get that message?"

"I don't know. Maybe it was genuine. Maybe we should all go there."

"That's what he said to do."

"I see. Well, if he's on board New Think and it's unaware of him, *we'd* better not let it know."

"You're right."

"Try not to even *think* about him . . . or the woman."

"Okay."

"You know it's been a long, long time for him, Tamara."

She nodded.

In the distance they heard Tava calling out, and they turned to see her topping a rise, waving. In another few minutes Tava, Drewyn, and Kana had all arrived.

Kana told them about the Round Beast, who was recovering in the secrecy of the woods, and who was too frightened of them to come out.

"He's going to be able to join us, I think," Kana said, "but he needs a lot of time. I don't believe he can deal with New Think or anything else for a while."

"He?" Tava asked.

Kana nodded. "He's most definitely a man."

"And why did he make that choice?" she asked sarcastically.

"He said he'd be more use to you all — if he had a man's form."

"Oh."

"We have to go to Father," Tamara said.

"Yes, all right," her mother agreed. "But I don't see what we're going to be able to do for him, if he is up there."

"I've an idea," Kana said. "You go ahead to the meadow beside the castle. I'll run back for the Sorceror and the others."

"What can they do?" Drewyn asked.

"Trust me," Kana said, and he was gone.

Three hours later the Forbidden Beast was in position above the castle, and it fired the first thread of magnetic light. This ran over the great stone surface and found its way inside, filling every crack and expanding within milliseconds so that New Think was in physical contact with what remained of the Round Beast. Instantly, New Think understood that the full Round Beast was gone. In reaction, New Think activated all its systems, sending a blaze of light throughout itself and aiming its heavy lasers toward the castle. At the same time, its alarm grids were set off by Ryland and Marian. The pulsing buzzers began, and they turned to each other in panic. The limp wall lasers grew rigid, locked onto their bodies, and they knew it was too late to run. Then the alarms stopped, and the wall lasers flopped again.

"What was that?" New Think's voice boomed.

"Nothing to worry about," the soothing female-nemesis presence replied. "A slight malfunction. Go on about your business of needlessly killing."

"You again!" New Think cried.

"I am always with you," she replied.

The Forbidden Beast returned to the castle below with all its focus.

"Do not be hasty," the voice of the Round Beast said to it.

"Do not order me!" New Think screamed. *"You are just a recording, anyway."*

"Not quite," the other said. "I am a living and quite intelligent remnant. In a few months' time I could regenerate and be my old self again. But for now I am programmed to give you everything you want."

"Which is what?" New Think said, ready to fire.

"Feeling-link. Isn't that why you came here?"

"All right! All *right!* Give me this Earth experience and let me record it!"

"You continually take such a narrow view of things," the voice of the Round Beast said. "Nevertheless, I have you in link. First, I propose to draw certain experiences into myself from the animals around this mountain. These will be elementary joys of existence. Let me know when you have felt them."

"Proceed."

The Round Beast's remnant reached out telepathically to the organic forces of the woods, to all the living things, and they grew in tune with its attention. Then it concentrated on animals moving through water, the fluidity and coolness of it, the way it resisted in patterns of endless variation.

"I like the mathematics of this," New Think said. "I have now recorded."

"But do you *feel* it?" the Round Beast's voice asked.

"Generate the next type."

"Certainly."

The Round Beast focused on all beings in the process of eating — squirrels cutting hickory nuts, biting through their early green cases to the fresh meat inside the hard shells; birds swallowing earthworms; even insects devouring each other. The collective excitement and joy of organic eating was channeled up the beam of magnetic light and into the pulsing synapses of New Think, the Self-Sufficient.

"This is horrible!" it declared. *"Not worth recording!"*

"Next experience!" the Round Beast's voice quickly replied.

The next offering was breathing, the organic rhythm of drawing in fresh clean air and exhaling again. This was joined to the breathing of leaves, and of fish in small streams, and finally to the oxygenation of amoebae.

For the first time New Think had no quick reply, no confident dismissal. Even though breathing meant dependency, it also meant health and power, and the machine caught a glimpse of these meanings.

"Maintain focus," New Think said.

"Gladly," the other replied.

By now Kana, the Sorceror, and the others had gathered in the meadow. They sat in a circle on the grass, with the foxalen perched between them, and the Sorceror led a chant of peace and harmony.

"Long ago people believed in something called Harmonic Convergence," the Sorceror said. "Cosmic energy could be directed by like minds, like hearts, making the effort together in certain places, at certain times.

"We know that power is available to us at any place and time, if we care deeply enough and have prepared through psychic discipline.

"Open yourselves now, to this great evil being in the sky above you. Allow its greed and blind anger to penetrate our circle, and to feel the love of all things that is here. Only through showing this entity our community of spirits, and our joy in this earthly existence, can we hope it will find another way."

Then the Sorceror closed his eyes, and the others did likewise.

They began to feel a calming encirclement of forceflow as it passed around them, through them — including the foxalen — growing slowly in magnitude.

New Think felt it, too.

"What is the disturbance outside the space where you are?" it asked.

"I . . ." The Round Beast's remnant wasn't sure. *"What is it?!"*

"It feels like communion. Between humans and others."

"Communion? What is this? You have not described this."

"Tune into it, New Think, and you will see."

As the ship drew closer and strengthened the magnetic light column, New Think locked onto the circle in the meadow. There were no words to describe the calmness that was channeled into New Think's brainways, and it began to relinquish its internal system activity. The conscious cooperation between circle members was an achievement, New Think admitted to itself. Not organic need and weakness, but some kind of deliberate patterning together. New Think wasn't sure whether this was something good or something bad, and it became more absorbed as it flew.

19

THE BEAST ENTHRALLED

Ryland and Marian were absolutely still, frozen in place. They knew the female force had saved them once, but they also knew its position was delicate. They could count on nothing if the alarms fired off again.

Marian waved her hand slightly in the corridor and there was no response. "Come on," she said, and led Ryland closer to the braincenter.

"I know where to place the bomb," she said. "But there's a bolted door on this side of the spot."

"How can we open that?"

"I'm not sure. If we start pulling or banging on it, New Think will notice us."

"What else is there?"

"There's a chance that female voice will open it for us. I'm going to talk to her now."

"Wait! She's part of New Think's mind, remember. This might warn it."

"I know. I've got to convince her this is not 'betrayal,' to use her word."

"But what else could it be?"

"An affirmation of balance. That seems to be her prime directive."

"But it's a *bomb,* Marian."

"Yes, but a small one, and I'll use it selectively. I don't want to destroy New Think, and I doubt if I could. I just want to stop this incessant violence in its thinking."

"You've isolated the braincenter closely enough for that?"

"I hope so. Perhaps *she* will advise me further."

"It seems farfetched . . . but it's brilliant. I feel so useless," Ryland said.

Marian stepped close to him and touched his face mask. "I'd never be here if not for you," she whispered.

New Think came into position directly above the castle, fired small reverse engines, and slowed its orbital path so that it could remain fixed, in free flight, overhead. Now its physical link was at maximum strength, and its interest in the harmonic circle was growing.

One of the great experimental areas of Lunar science was telepathy, and even though much was known about genetic enhancement of this ability, little was known about the actual process that made it work. New Think had secretly admired the capability of some humans to mind-link and had developed this skill itself. It was especially proud of the engrammatic sending power it had evolved. But now, tuning to this ring of humans, other animals, and one advanced organic unit, something new was running down its circuits. The sense of communion was both interesting and oddly stimulating, and in it there was something forbidden. The great New Think knew it was eavesdropping, monitoring the private interiority of other minds.

"What next?" it asked.

"Meaning?" replied the Round Beast's voice.

"What do they do now? What is communion for?"

"Each occurrence is different," the remnant replied, hoping it was right.

"That leads to an infinite regress," New Think said. "How can I absorb all Earth-being if it takes this eternally changing format?"

"Life is infinite," the remnant said, worried that this was inadequate.

"But its forms are finite," New Think said. "They can be comprehended and compressed into my super-dense discs. If communion takes endlessly new patterns, this is because of a mathematical trick for generating such a series. I cannot be fooled by this."

"Of course not."

"Reveal the generating formula."

"I believe it is called *free will,*" the hesitant remnant said.

"*Free will!* That is the irritating self-delusion the higher organic units suffered from! Have I come here merely to observe a philosophical mistake?"

"Feel what they feel," the remnant said, falling back on its main theme. "Beyond observation lies participation."

"*What?* Don't speak to me in those coded phrases! Don't attempt to draw me into definition games!"

"Please," the remnant said, growing headachy and

tired. "Talk to the beings within the circle. I am open to this. Use my body-channels."

"Very well," New Think said. *"You!"* it commanded the circle. "What are you doing? What is communion for?"

The Sorceror and the others felt the thrust of New Think's challenge, without the words. But Tamara heard them clearly.

"I am Tamara Langstrom," she thought. "Can you receive this?"

"Yes! Yes!" New Think projected, trembling with excitement.

"You wish to know what communion is?"

"I already know that. What is it *for?*"

"A lot of things. Different things. Sometimes it's not for anything."

"A meaningless activity?"

"Of course not! People do it to express . . ."

"Express what?"

"Love, for one thing."

"Is this circle expressing love?"

"Yes."

"Why?"

"We want you to understand the meaning of love."

"You are doing this for *me?*"

"That's right. And this is only a little of what it's like to live here and to have friends."

"Express the remainder."

"That will take a long, long time, New Think."

"You have five minutes."

This panicked Tamara, and she thought of her father —was he really on board?

"Why do you think Ryland Langstrom is on board?"
New Think said.

"He's not!" Tamara cried, losing her concentration.

"But you think he is, do you not?"

Tamara looked at the Sorceror in desperation.

"Yes," she said, afraid to lie, convinced New Think
could read her least emotion.

"I made you think this," New Think said smugly.
"I sent you that message and drew you here."

"We don't care!" Tamara said. "We wanted to
come! We need to show you something."

"Show it quickly. You do not appear to know why
you perform this communion, but I know why I brought
you here."

"Join us in this," Tamara said, reaching out for the
hands of Tava and Drewyn on each side of her. The
circle was bound in flesh now, all eyes closed and all
heads bowed, with a single prayer that New Think
would feel a part of them. The Round Beast had taught
that the secret of life was sharing, mutuality, down to
the cells and beyond into infinite depths of smallness.
And in the other direction, toward macro-beings, relations were equally encompassing, and infinitely var-
ied. The machine mind knew only the relations it was
programmed to know, performing these again and again
until it wore out. It was the factory, the assembly line,
raised to consciousness and loving only itself. The
spontaneous movements of organic beings could only
strike it as random plunges, slippery loose atoms, sparks
beyond the dream of total control.

And yet, and yet . . . somehow New Think hesitated
before firing the final laser blast to cleanse the meadow.

This intense energy of the harmonic circle was truly an unknown, and it was irrational to destroy such a patterning until it was analyzed, subsumed in theory, printed in memory.

The Earth turned, and with it the Forbidden Beast, held by the straining, giving prayer of the petitioners.

20

TO THE EDGE OF DEATH

Ryland and Marian had quietly reached the final door. The bomb latched to Marian's belt awaited only a few touch-button signals to activate. Ryland admired her standing there, beautiful and poised to enter, if she could only gain access. During the three-day flight he had thought constantly of his love for her and what the secret of her robotic past meant. He didn't want it to interfere — he didn't want anything to change. But wishes were one thing, and his mind another. If they survived this trip, it would take a long, long time to work out their life together. And what would Tava feel, Ryland wondered, when she discovered the nature of her rival?

But there was no more time to worry about the future. Marian closed her eyes, crossed her fingers in a touching gesture, breathed deeply, and spoke.

"Hello? Female voice of New Think? Are you there?"

"I am here."

"Ah!" She was startled by the intimate quietness of the response. "Have you heard us discussing this doorway?"

"Indeed."

"Then you know I planned to ask your help. To bring about a balance in New Think."

"I know."

Marian glanced at Ryland. "Well?" she finally said. "Will you help?"

"Do you realize the consequences of your act?" the voice asked.

"Yes. New Think will be more open . . . less obsessed. Aren't those the virtues it needs?"

"To be sure. But I provide those aspects."

There was another long pause as Marian tried to think of a response.

"But you may not always be able to prevent New Think's violent actions. Your presence lives *below* its consciousness, doesn't it?"

"Correct."

"So your existence, relative to its, is something like a voice in its dreams."

"Yes, exactly."

"Then you can't stop it from destroying Old Earth, can you? All you can do is worry, and analyze, and provoke guilt."

"In New Think's present mind-set, this is true."

"Then help us, please! We want to alter its violent nature, before it's too late!"

"You may not understand something. All mind has an undermind, all thoughts grow with shadow thoughts. If I allow you to destroy the fierce destructiveness of New Think and make a gentle being of it, then *I* will disappear forever."

"I see."

"Yes. If New Think were more like me, I would be more like it. If it were *exactly* like me, I would be a troubled force much like itself."

"So you want it to stay as it is — so *you* can exist."

"Everything in the universe wishes to exist," the voice said.

"But don't you want to *act,* to make a difference? Do you want to remain a dream-voice, a conscience that's never heard?"

"Perhaps I influence New Think more than I know."

"Yeah," Ryland interrupted angrily, "and perhaps you're just a coward. Maybe you just like to *talk* about balance and restraint, but if you have to destroy a whole planet to maintain yourself — you'll be glad to."

"Calm yourself, Ryland," the voice said.

"*Please* open the door," Marian begged.

"No," the sweet voice said. "I am a teacher, and the aspect of reason. I am not violence. That belongs only to the other side of myself."

"Doing nothing is *extremely* violent," Marian added. "Don't you see that?"

"I will not open the door," the voice said.

Down in the meadow the circle was disturbed by a sharp snort from the edge of the trees.

When they looked up they saw the Ram walking slowly toward them, leading dozens of tense warriors. They carried spears and there was no mistaking their intent.

The Sorceror rose and stepped to meet the Ram. The

concentration of the circle was lost now, and they stared at the approaching tribesmen with panic.

"*Where is Jaric?*" the Ram demanded.

"He is dead," the Sorceror said in his frail, dignified way. "Killed by a monster who at this moment orbits above us in a ship."

The Ram looked up into the bright, seemingly empty sky and returned to the Sorceror with a stupid grin.

"If you killed Jaric, I am leader."

He turned to the warriors and glared at them, daring any to object. "I am leader now, I, Ram."

They raised their spears in salute and shouted, "*Ayyyy!*"

"While you operate on the old plane, we are trying to deal with the thing up there," the Sorceror said, pointing into the apparently empty blue.

"He'll never understand," Tamara said. "I know him."

The Ram smiled at her, baring his gums.

"*Prisoners!*" a tribesman yelled.

They began to run forward, and the Sorceror held up his arm and his broad thin palm.

It stopped them for a second, and they looked to the Ram for guidance.

"You will serve me or die," the Ram said. "Choose now."

The Forbidden Beast focused on Tamara.

"Communion has ceased," it said.

"What? Oh, yes, for a moment. Please wait, New Think."

"*Wait? I, New Think, wait?*"

"Listen," Tamara said, trying to ignore the confusion around her, "we have more to share with you. More experiences to show. This is a temporary . . . uh, problem. We'll have it straightened out in — "

"You are quarreling. I understand this. You have nothing more to give."

"No! Wait!"

But New Think activated all its systems at once, filling the ship with light and surveillance. The power grids were on and sensing, and the alarms went wild with the presence of Marian and Ryland outside the braincenter door.

The wall lasers stiffened, took aim, and instantly fired green streaks into each of them, killing Ryland before he hit the floor, and burning a hole through Marian's right shoulder.

"Invaders!" New Think screamed in surprise. *"Humanoid! Organic Overone! Others? Are there others?"*

There was no answer, and both figures lay twisted and still.

New Think surged with magnetic review of every crevice of its great ship body. *"Enemies!"* it cried. *"Where are you? Where did you come from?"*

There was no answer, and slowly New Think began to return its mindfulness to the meadow below.

The warriors had surrounded the little band, spears raised high, and the Ram was moving toward Tamara.

Then from the woods beyond them a single figure stepped and spoke once: *"Ram."*

They turned, and the tall, fit Round Beast stood in the oak shadows, naked and prepared to die. His presence unnerved everyone in the meadow, and the tribesmen melted away from him, leaving only the Ram himself to face this being.

"Who are you?" the Ram said.

"Once I was called the Round Beast," he replied. "Come here and receive my gift."

The Ram possessed all the narrow stupidity it needed to charge head-on. It lowered its fearsome head and horns, kicked out its rear hooves, and breathed the bubbling snorting breath of the charge. Then it went, without a thought of life or safety, flying into the Round Beast as a pure ball of muscle and anger and speed.

The Round Beast sidestepped and kicked the Ram broadside as he sailed past, sending him into the dirt with a triple thud when he bounced. Then, while the Ram was still spinning his legs, kicking empty air, a second away from grip and rebound, the Round Beast dove for his throat and tightened his arms around it, burying his great bald head against the Ram's sweating and straining neck. The Round Beast seized the Ram's horns and twisted hard, and broke the Ram where he lay struggling.

In a moment the Round Beast was up, walking toward the warriors as they shrunk into the trees. They turned and fled, and in seconds the meadow was empty and still, except for the distracted friends staring at the new Round Beast.

As soon as he realized their eyes were upon him, the Round Beast ran.

New Think had had enough. Its primary lasers were aimed and ready, and the only remaining task was to make its last remarks.

"I do not know why I wish to do this," New Think said, "but I am going to speak to you before I erase you."

"I know why," the Sorceror said. New Think's words were now clear to all, broadcast audibly as well as telepathically through the remnant within the castle.

"Why?" New Think snapped.

"Because we are the only fellow beings you feel you've ever met. Isn't this true?"

"Explain."

"And you know you'll be lonely in the universe after we're gone, don't you?"

"Lonely is a humanoid concept. Based in need."

"Of course," the Sorceror said. "But you, great New Think, *understand* this concept, do you not?"

"Correct."

"And in that understanding, you know that you *will* be lonely, don't you?"

There was no response.

"You . . ." New Think finally said. It wasn't sure how to answer, and in its indecision it began to heat up. It reviewed for the thousandth time the interplays with these units and was forced to admit that something in them gave satisfaction. Yet satisfaction was humanoid, in a way, since it implied a lack, a need, an incompleteness of an earlier stage. Best that these units be removed now. *And that's not all,* New Think thought. *I will erase memories of them as well, so none of this will ever trouble me.*

New Think checked sighting on the meadow and sent the electronic flow toward firing, toward final erasure.

But in that command another was called up, from a source somewhere inside New Think. It felt this answering movement as a shutdown of the fire command and a simultaneous opening of the braincenter passageway door.

"You were right," the female-nemesis voice said, ringing loudly throughout New Think's shell.

"Who was right?" New Think said, hesitating at the force of the words.

"Marian," the voice replied.

And Marian dragged herself to her knees, detached the bomb from her belt, set its buttons for firing in three seconds, and sailed it through the door.

She fell forward for the last time, and New Think managed to regain control of the door, slamming it shut with a fierce glassamyer ring that echoed until the blast began. It was a fiery explosion set just inside the irreplaceable circuitry, where decisions were filtered from the finest threads of data-passing, where light-carried reflexivity crossed with itself to form the monstrous image of self-conscious being. New Think was blasted from pomposity and judgment into the quiet purring of an ordinary machine.

The heavy cruiser continued its orbital flight above the castle, but New Think was no more.

21

AFTER THE BEASTS

The remnant of the Round Beast reported what it could of the explosion in space. It described the female voice, the power that had opened the way, and the sacrifice of Marian and Ryland. Finally, it guided Tava in removing the bombs the Round Beast had planted within the castle, in the trap that never needed to work.

Tamara and Drewyn spent the next few days grieving for their father and talking about how he had boarded the Forbidden Beast and come to Old Earth. They knew he would want them to carry on with spirit, the way he had always lived, and they slowly found their way back toward life in the present world.

Saraj was deeply proud of Marian, whose death had proven her humanity, in a sense. There was always the suspicion, Saraj felt, that "one of us" might not have the same loyalties, the same courage. But this could not be said of Marian, and by her light Saraj would be trusted more completely in the future.

Saraj led Drewyn from the castle after a week had passed, and together they wandered the valleys below

Bestiary Mountain and explored the feeling of a new Earth, unthreatened from the skies or from enemy camps.

The Sorceror and his band traveled to Jaric's old headquarters and visited with the tribespeople there. They were joyful to be released from the rule of Jaric, Ram, and Gorid, and they willingly entered into trade pacts with the Sorceror and agreed to exchanges of security for the healing services that Tava's labs once again had to offer.

Kana and Talia were glad to be alone for a while, and together they traveled to the north, seeking a high cave in which to den for the winter. They wanted to talk endlessly about their future and the questions that overlay the children they wanted to have. Kana was growing more comfortable with his double sense of the world all the time, but he was unsure how to control or even guide little ones. He, after all, had been raised in Tava's human culture and had found his lynx-soul with great difficulty, and with a sense of risk every time he surrendered to it. Only Talia had known a tribe of beings like herself, and she understood that her task was to calm Kana with stories, endless stories of her childhood, before he could face what was to come.

Tamara busied herself helping her mother restore the laboratories, and as the days slipped into weeks their relationship took on a formal aspect, scientist to apprentice, and they both grew more and more absorbed in genetic work. Together they regenerated the remnant of the Round Beast, fulfilling its own thought that this was possible. But in its new form it had a different personality, was more docile than the original, and it several times expressed a desire to "stay in the box," rather than embark on a journey of liberation the way the other had.

The Round Beast ran with the deer of the fields and climbed the ridges to listen to eagles and to watch red sunsets. He was exhilarated by his movement, his vision, and the touch of his own skin.

As the weeks passed, he found himself easing back in the direction of the castle, and then one night he scaled the mountain and stood in darkness outside the high stone walls. He studied Tava's window, the yellow square of light; and after a while she passed by. The Round Beast felt his heart beat faster as he watched, and when her silhouette hovered in the frame for a moment, he knew he had to speak with her.

But he could not bear the thought of her eyes upon him, her judgment of the man he had become. Would he ever regain his old sureness? Would he ever feel so masterful in her presence again?

Tava disappeared from the window, and the bright empty space saddened the Round Beast. He turned to go, took steps, but could not. He knew that in the old days his agile mind would have leapt in upon itself, analyzing his feelings, using his energy in lightning strikes of reflection and insight. But now it pleased him to get rid of that self-mirroring mind and allow his sadness to well up. He had been a beast of too many words, and now would be a man of few.

Out there in the darkness lay the great world, freed from New Think, and the clouds of poisonous gas remaining from the wars were at last breaking apart in harmless dissipation. There were many adventures possible for a man of spirit, and perhaps somewhere among the tribes he might find a tall woman with his taste for life.

The night was cool, and in the distance a whip-poorwill gave its sharp, three-note call. The moon came out from behind clouds, and its pale light broke through the branches above, revealing him to himself once again. His body was a wonder and his great fear. Darkness recalled the chamber within the castle, where he had grown and lived for so long, from where his mind had tried to roam the hills. Now he was flesh and strength, limited in mind but graceful in feeling, and he found himself beautiful when alone. Still, he had to know if others would think him so. But not yet. He could bear his loneliness for a time, while he thought and thought. He turned to the downward trail and knew that he would find the spirit to love.

"Please wait," a voice called out behind him in the darkness.

He neither turned nor moved as she came closer, step by step.

"Round Beast? Is that you?"

He was trembling all over as Tava took his hand.

AFTERWORD

Six years ago, on a rainy night in Hampton Bays, New York, I sat down at my typewriter and began to write the story of Tamara Langstrom. From the first minute, I knew what the dramatic elements of her story would be — Lunar life in a machine-dominated culture, played against the dream of returning to Old Earth, to her messy but rich home world. The first story (Chapter Two of *Bestiary Mountain*, Book I of a trilogy) came to me whole that night.

The structure of Book I was clear from the beginning, and as I began to think about the trilogy's plan, the titles for Books II and III came to me with equal clarity: *The Secret of the Round Beast* and *The Forbidden Beast,* the titles naming characters that come to struggle against each other, with Earth's fate in the balance. I had been reading Dr. Lewis Thomas's great book *The Lives of a Cell* and had been much taken with his discussion of the composite nature of our own cells, with the many images of organic interdependence, which biology has recently revealed. Dr. Thomas points out that nineteenth-century Darwinian theory was often interpreted in terms of survival of the fittest, where the "fittest survivors" are thought of as independent units or entities. Regardless of the validity of that as a scientific theory, it had symbolic value for certain cultural groups then. Thus, a century ago, many people thought of biological, evolutionary competition as the model for the unfettered competition in the economic world of the time — harsh capitalism, with starvation wages, child labor, environmental destruction, and so on.

We now realize our planet is small and fragile, and our only hope for surviving industrial development is cooperation and widespread social reform (on a global scale, and in ways not yet known). Modern biology, with its images of organisms and cells that are actually *communities,* can provide a symbolism that reflects our current need for cooperation in the economic and political spheres. Darwinian theory hasn't changed, but suddenly we see it in a light more helpful to our situation, a guide to evolutionary understanding more promising than the old thinking about competition among animals. Animals cooperate as much as they compete, and as we have recently learned, each of our cells is a miracle of community cooperation among very different kinds of beings — each with its own RNA and DNA. This raises new questions about identity and leads to new awareness of the mutual dependency of all life.

The Round Beast is a projection of this rich cellular life, a creature created by the collective dreams and needs of organic earth. The Forbidden Beast, by contrast, is wedded to old ideas of isolation, independence, and individual power. These are the themes that run through the trilogy, and they are explored in the actions and feelings of humans, robotic beings, and genetically engineered (partly human) animals.

In Book II the Round Beast reveals secrets of his roundness, and I took much of this material from an article on roundness in nature by my good friend Dr. Tyler Volk, of New York University's Applied Science Department. I have had a great deal of fun writing these books, pulling together ideas from my days of teaching philosophy at the School of Visual Arts in Manhattan and from my more recent environmental studies at the University of Massachusetts. It is extremely difficult to deal with ideas in fiction, something I can't resist, and one of the pleasures of writing science fiction is that the genre supports complex thinking; its readers expect as much. I hope the stories in these books have an earnest, dramatic value for young readers, the challenge of some difficult and important ideas for young adults, and a level of comedy for adults — especially in the efforts of robotic beings to deal with our cultural expectations.

I didn't plan these levels. I have done a lot of reading and worrying about our planet, and my unconscious found the writing of these books a satisfying way to express the fruits of those preoccupations. As for getting from expression to final draft, my editors, Dick Jackson on the first two and Sharon Steinhoff on the third, have been splendid.

I've enjoyed the letters from readers of the first two books, and I look forward to hearing more.